WYOMING
TRAILS

Center Point
Large Print

Also by Lauran Paine and available from Center Point Large Print:

Sheriff of Hangtown
Prairie Empire
Man from Durango
Guns in Wyoming
The Plains of Laramie
Way of the Outlaw
Ute Peak Country
Gunman's Moon
Rough Justice

This Large Print Book carries the Seal of Approval of N.A.V.H.

WYOMING TRAILS

—A Western Story—

Lauran Paine

CENTER POINT LARGE PRINT
THORNDIKE, MAINE

This Circle Ⓥ Western is published by
Center Point Large Print in 2014 in co-operation with
Golden West Literary Agency.

First Edition
December, 2014

The text of this Large Print edition is unabridged.
In other aspects, this book may vary
from the original edition.
Printed in the United States of America
on permanent paper.
Set in 16-point Times New Roman type.

ISBN: 978-1-62899-379-0 (hardcover)
ISBN: 978-1-62899-385-1 (softcover)

Library of Congress Cataloging-in-Publication Data

Paine, Lauran.
  Wyoming trails : a western story / Lauran Paine. — First edition.
  pages ; cm
  ISBN 978-1-62899-379-0 (hardcover : alk. paper)
  ISBN 978-1-62899-385-1 (pbk. : alk. paper)
  1. Large type books. I. Title.
  PS3566.A34W96 2014
  813'.54—dc23
                                                    2014034337

WYOMING TRAILS

CHAPTER ONE

When the coach slowed, the cold became more intense, more congealing. The soldier in his great-coat moved a little, pulled off a mitten, fumbled at the side-curtain catch, worked it free, and peered out. His nostrils pinched down against the night air; his eyes watered. Beyond were a few flickering lights, orange-yellow, some buildings, maybe thirty in all, unpainted, slatternly looking. He let the curtain fall back.

Faint in the gloom across the coach the big girl was looking at him. He could make out the mouth and nose but her eyes were hidden in shadow. It didn't matter; he'd seen her eyes before, when she'd first got on. They were liquid dark eyes, soft as new silk and far apart, serene eyes, and impressionable, as was her large, full mouth. He leaned back.

"All these towns look alike," he said. "Frozen stiff."

"It *is* cold," she said with emphasis.

He nodded stolidly for a second, then stood up and began shaking off the big coat. His body nearly filled the coach. He had to bend far over and a knife blade of lantern light from outside shone briefly upon his face. An odd face, rugged and courageous enough but with an illusive childishness about it, a smoothness of texture, a fullness.

"Here," he said.

"Oh, no. . . ."

"Sure. I'm not cold. I mean my body isn't. Not inside this uniform. These things are made from real good wool. Your body doesn't get cold in them. Just my face gets cold."

She took the coat because he was thrusting it at her. She held it a moment, looking at him, then quite abruptly she moved to his side of the coach, sat down, and spread the garment over both their legs. Tucking it in on her side, she leaned back.

He caught some fragrance from her, heard the brake squeal, the chain harness drag, and when the coach crunched down to a walk, he was braced. When it stopped, lurched, he was ready. Beyond the side curtains men called in the sharp winter air.

"Do you get out here?" he asked.

"No, I'm going on up to Tico."

He twisted to look up at her close. "Do you live in Tico? I'm going there, too."

"Are you? No, I don't live there. My uncle used to live there. He died and I'm going up to sell his cabin, crate up what he had, and send it back home. . . . And his body."

"Where to?"

"Nebraska. My family lives in Nebraska."

"Oh," he said, settling back again, listening to the sounds of fresh horses being hitched up.

The door opened and two men squeezed in, bent far over to keep from striking their heads. Both peered uncertainly at the other two passengers. Both were bearded; both smelled of liquor. When the coach was in motion again, the newcomers rocked side-by-side across the tiny aisle. From time to time they took long swallows from a bottle until finally they both tilted their hats forward and settled back. They were warmly dressed and had a small buffalo robe that they tucked around their legs. The soldier looked unblinkingly at the bottle wedged between them.

"That must be good cloth," the girl said, looking at his sleeve.

He raised it. "Plenty times you're glad it's heavy this time of the year," he said, dropping the arm.

"I imagine." She studied his profile for a moment. "It was terrible, wasn't it?"

He looked around. Their faces were close enough for the steam of their breath to mingle. He looked away. "Terrible? Some of it was," he said simply, "and some of it wasn't." The brown, shiny neck of the whiskey bottle drew his attention back.

"Were you wounded?"

"At Antietam." The whiskey would be swishing. He wondered how much the bearded men had drunk.

"Oh," she said with tenderness in the sound.

He liked it. It reminded him of the old woman who had cared for him at the farmhouse while he'd waited for an ambulance wagon. Old and ugly, skinny-breasted and bent, she'd had the softest touch he'd ever known. It had disturbed him and he'd felt ashamed. It had quickened an old yearning, an empty pathos.

"Was it bad?"

"The wound?" He shook his head without taking his eyes off the whiskey bottle. "Not bad. More scared than hurt."

"It's so unfair. You're so young . . ."

She let it dwindle away unfinished, and for a while they rode in silence. The coach rocked, their shoulders rubbed, arms touched.

"My name's Sarahlee," she said. "Sarahlee Gordon."

"I'm Ryan Shanley. They call me Shan."

"You look so young . . ." The rest of it was lost when one of the bearded men began to snore.

He turned to gaze at her. "I'm twenty-eight," he said, and made a smile, slow and infectious, that made him appear years younger. "You look kind of young yourself."

"Three years younger," she said, "but you don't look twenty-eight."

His smile died slowly. He gazed steadily at her, at the straight nose, the wide, dark eyes, the chestnut hair that showed below her hat around the temples, and at her heavy lips, at the ripe swelling of them, cold and scarlet. She got red and spoke quickly.

"You don't look more than twenty. When I first got on, I thought I was older than you were."

He shook his head without speaking. He was thinking of her mouth and the old woman's touch, confusing one with the other and feeling ashamed again but thrilled, too. She wasn't looking at him now.

"Does your family live in Tico?" she asked.

He moved, reached down, and tucked the greatcoat under his legs. "I don't have any family. I got a piece of land up there. Bought one piece and got another one adjoining through the Soldier's Bounty Act." He looked up. "I've never been in Tico in my life. In fact, I've never been in Wyoming before . . . and if it's always this cold, I'll take the dawn coach back, too."

She grinned. "It's cold anywhere in winter. Wyoming's the most heavenly place on earth in the summertime."

He leaned back and their shoulders met and rubbed. "Do you know Wyoming pretty well?"

"I used to spend a month or two each summer with my uncle at Tico. I know that country pretty well." She rolled her head sideways. "What made you take up land there if you've never seen the country?"

He regarded his mittens. "There were some soldiers in the hospital from up there," he said. "They kept telling me about it. I figured one place

11

was as good as another and maybe Wyoming . . . being so far away . . . might be the place to put down roots."

"There are opportunities," she said. "I suppose it would appeal to men, but there are still Indians there."

"Indians. . . . Who cares about Indians?" He was rubbing his hands together.

She looked at his face for a moment, then lowered her eyes and watched the way he rubbed his hands together. The night was stiff with cold. Outside, iron tires crunched over frozen earth. It finally got cold enough to seep through the side curtains and chill his flesh. He looked over where the two men now slept, fastened his glance upon the bottle between them. Finally he bent far forward, got the bottle, took three big gulps, drove the cork down with the palm of one enormous hand, and put the bottle back. Sarahlee was expressionless.

The whiskey kindled new fire in his stomach and out into his bloodstream to fingers and toes. Even his ears felt warm and red. He sighed and leaned back.

"Two square miles of land," he said. "Two whole square miles of it. Know what I'm going to do? Put a cabin right in the middle of it." He rolled his head to look at her. His breath was spicy. "Hibernate. Not talk to anyone, not see anyone, not hear anyone."

She smiled with her mouth. "You'll get tired of being a hermit."

"Not the way I feel right now I won't."

"I understand."

He kept on looking until she averted her face, then he closed his eyes. He didn't open them until dawn, and she was talking to him, rubbing his hands. His head lay against her shoulder. It was soft and fragrant there.

"We're in Tico," she said, and rubbed his hands more vigorously. "You'd better wake up."

When she moved her shoulder away, he blinked and straightened up, rubbed his face, and smiled at her. "Thanks. I expect I'd have slept for a month." He found his hat in his lap, put it on, felt stiff and cramped, sat back to relax for another moment or two, and watched her. Their thighs still touched under the greatcoat; it was a delicious sensation, made him think again of the old woman, her gentle hands, how he'd wanted to embrace her some way, not necessarily *that* way—sort of hold onto, sort of crawl into and never leave—that kind of a feeling.

She tucked her hair under the tiny hat with both hands. It thrust her bosom out sharply in the cold, pale light. She was a big girl. "If you don't know anyone here," she was saying with her face averted, "I'll be at my uncle's place . . . anyone can tell you where the Gordon cabin is. Come see me. Maybe I can help you get acquainted."

When she left him on the plank walk with steam all around them from their breath, from the horses, and on the store windows, he felt like someone had emptied the world of companionship. He watched her walk away, leaving that void behind. He stood there until the horses were led away, the baggage unloaded, the little clutch of men hastening toward the stage office and the stove. It was like his first day in the Army. Surrounded by people, noise and activity, and more alone than ever.

Beyond the town was emptiness. Far out under a low gray sky were gaunt mountains with dirty snow upon them. The heavens were lead-belly gray and the ground looked like it was contorted with pain, glistening with frost that could have been sweat on a forehead, upon an upper lip, its face rigid, ashen-looking.

He saw a saloon. People moved thinly around him. The bite of winter was numbing. Human breath hung, quivering in the cold. He went into the saloon, found it warm and rank-smelling. The men loafing there were rough-looking and hard-talking. Their behavior, like their attire, was rude, and he found their Wyoming whiskey like swallowing rasps. He drank it and choked, coughed. He set his bag down and blew his nose. Some of the water was drawn away from his eyes. Down the bar several feet a huge, shaggy-headed man gazed at him steadily. He ignored the man and ordered another drink, downed it, and that time controlled the choking but it cost an effort.

The bearded man snickered, then laughed with his head back. "Well," he said in iron merriment, "an Abe Lincoln boy who ain't got guts for Green River Lightnin'."

Out of the corner of his eyes Ryan Shanley saw a few saturnine smiles. The whiskey flowed moltenly in his blood. "Been busy lately," he said carelessly to the big, bearded man, "fixing it so's stay-at-homes could have the time to learn about drinking this stuff."

There was no particular animosity in the words but a fingernail of sharp steel picked at civilian consciences. The smiles died away. The bearded man's face grew blank and unpleasant, his stare brittle and appraising. Without relinquishing the hold he had on a whiskey glass, he said: "Didn't you get enough fightin' in your war, bluebelly?"

Shanley pushed his glass away. The heat and fumes were making him perspire. He felt as limp and oily-muscled as all outdoors, as big and invincible. He wore a mirthless little smile.

"I still got a little in me, whiskers," he said, "if you want to dig around to find it."

The bearded man nodded slightly, gently. "Any day," he said.

Ryan Shanley moved easily, threw a big looping blow the bearded man lacked the wits to dodge. He went over flat on his back, rolled over, got

15

up as far as his knees, and looked like a gut-shot bear down on all fours.

Chairs rattled back, men crowded up making noise, their breath preceding them. The stench of whiskey, horses, sweat, and damp clothing hung in the warm atmosphere. When the bearded man was back on his feet and unsteady, a stocky bartender worked through the press of bodies. His face was expressionless and he held a whittled wagon spoke in one hairy fist, but before he could get close enough, the bearded man had fumbled under his rider's coat and come up with a pistol. Ryan Shanley struck him again, as he was cocking the weapon, and that time he stayed down.

The fire dwindled in Shanley's brain. He stood there, looking downward, watching the bearded man scrabbling at the floorboards with crooked fingers, and knew he had been drunk. It made him feel a little ashamed. The barman pushed him roughly away. He listened with his head down to what the barman was saying.

"Want to fight, go outside. Y'had your drink, soldier, better move along now."

He went back out into the bitter cold, found the hotel, got a room, and bedded down. When he awoke, there was a dazzling sun in his face and his right hand ached. Two knuckles were skinned. He washed and went back outside. The morning air was cold but crystal-clear, the sun dazzling, eyes watering, he could see as far as the curve of the world. While the sun gave off no warmth, it felt good nevertheless. He rented a horse at the livery barn, saying he might return within a few hours and he might not return for several days, asked the liveryman where his land lay, got the directions, and rode north out of Tico.

There was a deceptiveness to the land. It looked like it slanted upward but actually it was flat. "Go north," the liveryman had said, "till you come to a tree with brands burned into the trunk . . . west from there to a two-story house, the Muller place. Beyond that you'll be on this land you're talking about."

The ground was frozen; his horse's hoofs made a sharp, loud sound magnified by the stillness. As he rode, his mind leaped from one thought to another, and when he got to the tree, there was a roll of land where he got down, flexed his arms and legs, and looked back the way he had come. Tico showed as a tiny blotch in the milky flow of country. Out a ways was a crooked, broad river. Farther still were forests, purple, forbiddingly dark. He groped for the bulky bag of shag, the thick packet of papers, rolled a cigarette like he'd learned to do from the Reb prisoners, smoked a moment with the congealing cold on his face, and squinted into the brilliant sun smash. Before going on again he drew a small bottle of whiskey from a coat pocket, uncorked it, drank deeply, and replaced it in the pocket. Warmth returned.

Maybe he'd done right. His eyes moved over the immensity of country. Maybe Wyoming wasn't such a bad place in spite of the cold. It was big, bigger than anything he could remember seeing or imagining. Bigger than the North and South rolled into one. Quiet, too. Quiet and still and new. He turned north and led the horse along behind him.

CHAPTER TWO

When he saw the two-story house there was a dark spiral of smoke rising straight up from its solitary narrow chimney. He looked at the house and smiled, opened his mouth and laughed without making a sound. It was square, tall, ludicrously city-like in its frozen setting of emptiness. There wasn't another house as far as anyone could see. Nothing, just barren land, just Wyoming sprawling north and east and west, rising a little here, flat as the palm of his hand there, tilted on end elsewhere. Open, timbered like a ten-year growth of whiskers, or brushy as could be. Slanted, flat, rolling, precipitous—Wyoming land, land, land. It made him feel tiny. He stopped walking when a herd of buffalo, far out, caught his attention with movement. He shook his head at their smallness—specks crawling over a huge prostrate body, naked and white with dead frost.

18

In all this void stood that two-story house. He got back into the saddle and rode toward it with his grin. A dog let off one startled yelp and fled toward the log barn. There were banks of white snow around the shaded corners of the house, a dirty, trodden path from house to barn. The stillness was crushing. He dismounted heavily and waited, stood there with reins in his hands not feeling like he ought to break that great depth of silence. Then a door slammed around in back, the report as sharp as a pistol-shot in the cold air. A burly, squat man hove into view, shrugging into a sheepskin coat. He had coarse gray hair, a seamed, blunt face, and small blue eyes. He nodded without a smile as he approached. Shan noticed his nose was prominent and hooked. When he was closer, Shan could see coffee and tobacco stain on a skimpy mustache.

"Good day, mister," Muller said, gazing fixedly at Ryan Shanley's face towering above him. "Not many soldiers up here this time of the year."

"Good day, sir."

Muller gestured with a thick arm. "You looking for soldiers? They're farther out, westerly."

Shan shook his head. "I'm not looking for any soldiers," he said. "I've seen all I ever want to see of them." He rummaged in a pocket with a stiff hand, fingers slid over the smooth glass of the little whiskey bottle, found the soiled scrap of paper that he drew out and unfolded. "Can you tell me where this land is?"

Muller bent to look. Shanley's sharpened sense of smell caught the scent of smoked meat, whiskey, horses, and cattle. Muller traced out the lines with a spatulate finger, then looked up. "Sure, I know that land well." He turned, screwed up his face and motioned with his arm. "Follow the road north. A mile from here you'll come to a juniper tree that's got a blaze on the side of the trunk, facing the road. The blaze is an old trail marker. That's the southwest corner of this here land." Muller ran a thick finger down the paper again, then let his arm drop to his side. "Rest of it's about squared-off from there, runs easterly. There's over two miles of it, mostly northeasterly. You can square it up by riding between the markers. Did you buy it?"

Shanley folded the paper carefully and pocketed it. "Part of it," he said. "The rest I got on the Soldier's Bounty Act."

"Well, well," Muller said, then lapsed into momentary and thoughtful silence. After a while he gestured toward Shan's horse. "Tie him up and come in for a spell. Maybe you ain't eaten yet. By the way . . . what's your name?"

"Shan . . . Ryan Shanley." He tied the horse to a stud ring in a bare tree and struck his mittened hands together.

"I'm Otto Muller. Let's get by the stove."

They entered the house. Mrs. Muller was as broad as her husband. Her features were heavy and impassive except for the eyes and mouth that showed a force and patience adding up to wisdom. She acknowledged Shanley's presence with a smile, set another place at the table without speaking, and herded both men close to the stove. Otto Muller hung his coat over the back of a chair and motioned for Shan to sit.

The house was like the people, Shanley thought, square, sturdy, unimaginative, built for durability, for great strength. Its furnishings were the same; everything was functional. When they ate the noon meal, the food was heavy and nourishing, and after the meal was over Muller went to an understair closet dark as a tomb and brought back a crockery jug that he set resoundingly upon the table.

"Two glasses, Mama."

She brought them, thick and heavy, of cloudy, imperfect glass. Muller sat down and pushed the jug toward Shanley. "Better'n fire wood," he said, eyes twinkling.

They drank and talked. Muller had been in Wyoming seven years. His long-dead father had emigrated from Silesia in 1838. Otto and his wife had never had any children. He said it in solemn tone and his wife did not look up from where she was slicing cabbage and listening. Then Muller brightened, seemed to turn away from his own past and peer at Shan.

21

"I thought soldiers liked girls and towns . . . there ain't much like that around here."

Shan smiled. He was warm and full and beginning to feel drowsy. "Not towns," he said, and Muller laughed in understanding. "I don't care if I never see another town." He sipped the whiskey. "This is good. You make it?"

"I buy it from an Indian trader. Well, what're you going to do with all that land?"

"Go to ranching, I expect."

Muller's eyebrows went up a little. "Soldier-rancher? You know anything about it, about cattle, horses, haying, ranch work?"

"I'll learn," Shan said.

"It's hard work."

Shan shrugged carelessly.

Mrs. Muller spoke then. "There's nothing to live in out there."

Shan stood up. His mouth curved upward. "I've lived like a hog for four years, expect I can stand it for another year or so."

Otto Muller also arose. "I'll help you put up a cabin," he said. His eyes were watering a little and there was splotchy dark color in his face. He gestured more than usual as he spoke. "You got plenty timber up there. We'll make a cabin and maybe a barn."

Shan protested. "You've got your own chores. Besides, what'm I to you? Just a soldier rode in is all."

"Hah! This is winter. Nothing much to do in winter, feed a little, drink a little to keep warm, chop wood, trap maybe. You ride up there, take a long look around, then come back. Supper'll be ready."

When Shan rode away from the Muller place, the sun was slipping off into the West. He saw the faces watching from a window and waved. He felt good. He also felt drunk. Good people. He didn't laugh at the two-story house now. Fine people for neighbors. Otto'd said something about some other folks living farther out, beyond his land, but he'd only half heard. Anyway, Otto hadn't said very much about them, only that they lived beyond. It didn't matter.

He rode in as nearly a northerly line as he could and found the witness tree. After that it was his—whichever way he rode, east, north, or back southward, it was his—and in its nakedness, its gray dismalness, it was Shanley's empire. He rode at random across it until the sun sank with surprising swiftness, the cold closed down with its weighted and bitter silence, then he dismounted, beat his hands together, and looked out from a little knoll. He was aware of the booming silence, the inert and brooding distances that surrounded him.

He would make a ranch here—become a rancher. He laughed out loud. The horse turned and looked at him. A rancher! From a slum-corner orphanage in New York's grime and soot to the Army. From four years of soldiering to the Land of Tall Grass—Otto said the Indians called it that, Land of Tall Grass. This endlessness, stillness, loneliness. It bore in on him, worked its way into his soul, into his spirit—his loneliness. That big girl, that Sarahlee Gordon. Not loneliness. A man's mother would have looked like that when she was young and ripe. A man's mother would look like that old woman down South when she got old. Like Otto Muller's wife in the mid-years. Femaleness, comforting, something warm and smotheringly fragrant. Femaleness—and shame. The longer he thought and stood there, the more vividly could he picture Sarahlee. Big, voluptuous, strong, white flesh, lips parted a little, giving, straining to give. Rubbing his hands in the coach. Rubbing his chest, his shoulders, and his back while his head lay upon her shoulder.

A big vein at the side of his throat pulsed. He'd had boyhood dreams of a mother like that, of an abundantly female woman. Later, in the Army, he'd even seen women like that—and different, too, but still women. He hungered and craved and felt ashamed. With Wyoming under his feet, in his eyes, in his nostrils, sharp and tangy and ice-cold, two square miles of it he could have a big girl—in the Land of Tall Grass such a thing could be.

He turned his head with the swelling in his neck and the great pound of his heart like thunder.

He'd build the cabin near those trees; there'd be shade there and shelter. Where that fanned-out clearing was he'd put the barn, the big, big barn to match his dreams. He'd get cattle, horses, a wagon, some tools, he'd build and let the pulse of this earth seep in deep—and he'd get the girl.

He stood there until the horse moved, shifted its weight, then he turned toward it, mounted, and started back for the road. He was exhilarated. It wasn't Muller's whiskey either; the cold had sucked that artificial heat out of him hours before. There was a meaning to existence, something beyond day-to-day living, eating, drinking, swearing, living in mud, and sleeping. Sleeping. . . . He writhed in the saddle.

The road was empty; shadows lay, sharp and stark-edged, along it. Dusk was curtaining the world with unexpected suddenness. He didn't heed it. There were fumes in his head, fragrant scents intermixed, Sarahlee and the cold, dark smell of frozen earth.

Otto, returning toward the house from milking, stopped and watched him approach. There was the steaming bucket in his fist and a thoughtful pensiveness in his small, candid eyes. When he called out, the words carried with brittle distinctness over a thousand yards.

"Put the horse in the barn an' fork him some hay. Supper'll be ready the time y'get in."

Shan unsaddled, unbridled, tied the horse, and

loaded his cribbed manger. The odors of other animals were rich around him. Nostalgic, too, although he'd never been around animals much. He stood in the doorway a moment, watching an early moon come up, white with an illuminating rind of ice, chaste-looking, as lonely as God. The air hurt his nose, was bitterly cold inside him. Other nights, in warmer climates, he'd seen that big moon all silver-sad. Here its coldness made it different; more aloof, less personal, less concerned with the doings of man. He liked it better this way. Big, round, firm, aloof—you couldn't reach up and touch it. Like the girl, like Sarahlee Gordon. He moved away from the barn.

At the house Mrs. Muller smiled at his blue lips, red cheeks, and wet eyes. She had a joke inside her at his expense.

"Cold?"

Shan grinned. His teeth were large and even, big and strong like the rest of him. "Cold all right," he told her, shedding his hat and great-coat. "A clean cold, I don't mind it."

"You'll get used to it," Otto said from the table. His grizzled hair was brushed flat, his face shiny from scrubbing. "In the winter here you spend most of your time keeping warm, doing what's got to be done and waiting for summer." He used both hands expansively to wave Shan to a chair at the table. "In the summer you got no time for thinking or planning . . . just working . . .

so in the winter you plan and try to keep warm."

From the crackling stove his wife said: "You saw a lot of the war?"

Shan sat down. " 'Sixty-One to 'Sixty-Five," he said. "I saw my share of it." He stared at Otto a moment, on the verge of saying something he never said. Otto returned the look. Something passed between them then, something masculine, and when the meal was nearly finished, Otto brought out the whiskey jug. Shan noticed Mrs. Muller accepted this as a natural thing and it pleased him. Plain people, the Mullers, honest, plain people.

Otto poured the glasses full and talked of cattle, horses, Indians, the weather, Tico, the neighbors, and the past. Words flowed from him as easily as water, as naturally as air. In the things he said and the way he said them Shan understood that Otto felt he was part of Wyoming. He also noticed both Mullers never asked personal questions, which pleased him. The Army had been cruelly inquisitive, indifferently unsympathetic to orphandom, disinterested and disdainful after it had laid a man's soul naked, contemptuous.

Later Otto stood up and only the crackling of the stove broke the hush. "You stay here," he said to Shan, "until we get your cabin up."

His wife smiled approval in her quiet, reserved way. "Show him the room, Otto," she said. There was anticipatory pride in her voice, eagerness. Shan looked down at her. Otto thumped his shoulder and started away. Shan did not want to follow, didn't want to see the room. He felt embarrassed and confused. Otto rolled as he walked, massive shoulders overburdening the rest of his body.

"Come on. In here, Shan."

The bed was a real one not a wall bunk. There was a rag rug, four framed pictures of people who looked stern and rigid. There was even a maple rocker, scarred from the long wagon journey but solid as stone. The whiskey mood made Shan's eyes smart and burn. He bent, fisted one huge hand, and beat it several times into the pillow, hard.

"How do you like it, Shan?"

"Like it," he said, touching the rocker's back, looking at the grim people on the walls. "I never lived in anything like it, Otto, I can't. I've got to get back to Tico."

Otto laughed, a rich and hearty sound. He was immensely pleased; his wife beamed palely from the doorway. "I want to tell you something," Otto said from his flushed face. "I want to tell you Georgia and me got no family. For me that's all right, fer her it ain't. You understand?"

Shan didn't. He just stood there gazing at Otto.

"Well, it don't matter, Shan. But you got to stay here, see? We'll do things this winter. It'll be different than sitting around the damned stove all winter. We'll make a cabin up there."

"Otto, you don't want to do that. Man, it's cold up there."

"Well," Otto said, cocking his head to one side to look upward, and there was a smile in his little eyes. "Don't you *want* a cabin? You want to live in a teepee like an Indian and maybe freeze to death . . . freeze up solid, Shan?"

"No, of course I . . ."

"We'll do it, then, boy."

"Listen, Otto, it isn't up to you to look out for me."

"Hah! I got a reason. I got a real good reason for offering to do this. When it's time to mark my cattle, you'll be beholden, see? Say, how tall are you anyway?"

"Six feet four inches."

"Must weigh two hundred then."

"Two-twenty."

Otto wagged his head in admiration. "And young," he said. "I'm getting older . . . slower . . . you could wrestle a calf down like nothing. I need a neighbor like you. Understand now?"

Shan grinned. The sting was gone from his eyes but there was a big lump in his chest and he thrust out his hand. "You've got one," he said.

CHAPTER THREE

The arrangement turned out to be a godsend for Shan. Otto had two strong teams. He had tools and wagons, but more valuable than anything else he had wise and knowing hands. He could build anything, mend, overhaul, plan as though cabins and log barns and ranching were all he'd ever known in his lifetime. Shan learned from him, but slowly. Manual labor came easily but the rest of it—the joining of logs, the notching, fitting of joints, the figuring and scheming—came very slowly and some of it he could not grasp at all, but Otto had patience. He would explain and show him, then do it himself without a cross word.

Shan ached and sweated under the heavy clothing, and cursed wildly at times, became discouraged and occasionally said they ought to quit, but Otto instilled a dogged persistence with his words and actions. Shan kept on working.

When the snow grew blinding-deep and swirling with a fury, they'd putter around the Muller place, and in time Shan became accustomed to the eternal cold, the eye-hurting whiteness, the everlasting stillness that they broke with talk—man talk.

"Gordon? Yes, I recall him. Trapper, sort of. Old man with a shack on the edge of Tico."

30

"I rode here on the same stage with his niece."

Otto stopped working, leaned on a tie-stall partition, and watched Shan muck out. Beyond the glassless window lay a steaming rich mass of manure strong with ammonia scent.

"Oh," Otto said.

Mrs. Muller clanged the triangle. They went down to the house to clean up and eat. The day was mauve with a hint of storm yet to come. Inside, the stove hissed merrily, the kitchen smelled wonderfully of spices, of meat pie, fresh bread, and something that every household smelled of but that actually had no smell at all— home, belonging, family.

The cabin grew, but slowly because, in spite of Shan's eagerness and Otto's wisdom, the weather was defiant. It was tantalizing to see half a cabin, picture it as it must someday be, and not be able to hasten it. Otto laughed.

"When I was your age," he said, "I was like that . . . all impatience. Don't worry, we'll have it ready come spring."

"I shouldn't be living off you, Otto. I don't feel right about it."

"When you're fixed up here, you'll pay me back. You'll see." Otto worked all day making doors while Shan split shakes for the roof.

"Shan, you ever had trouble in your life?"

The axe in his hand slowed, dropped to a halt. "Trouble? Sure, who hasn't had trouble in their

31

life?" The axe rose, descended, and a shake fell away.

"I mean with pretty rough men."

"Sure, with them, too." The axe rose above the block of pine but stayed there. "What's on your mind, Otto?"

Otto removed his little black pipe and spat. "Something you don't know. The Blessing place is north of you. Art and Amos Blessing, brothers. They've used your land for range ever since they came out here. They probably won't like your taking it up."

"Well," Shan replied, "I'm not doing anything wrong."

"No, but folks are funny. They resent new-comers. The Blessings will."

Shan let the axe hit the block, watched the shingle fall away. "They're tough?"

"Yes," Otto said with finality, and returned to fitting the door. "They've got a reputation for being fast with their guns and even faster with their dislikes."

Shan said nothing. They worked until the early shadows came, then climbed into the wagon and set out for home. On the way Shan said: "If they don't know I'm here until spring, it'll be too late."

Otto shook his head. "That won't matter. They'll pay you a visit sooner or later. If you're living here, it won't make any difference to them, they'll try to make you fight."

Shan gazed at his red, chapped hands. "It won't be the first time I've had to fight," he said.

"With guns, Shan, with pistols? Not hand fighting. Men up here are pretty handy with pistols. They spend a lot of the winters practicing. The Blessings do. I've ridden up and seen them at it."

"I've used pistols," Shan said, "but not like that."

"That's what I thought," Otto said, and fell silent until they were back home, putting up the horses. "You got a pistol?" he asked abruptly.

"Well, I've got a Derringer, but not one of those horse pistols."

"You've got to get one. A carbine, too. Even if you never have trouble with the Blessings, you've got to have a pistol and a carbine around the place."

"Next time I go to town," Shan said. "Got to get down there one of these days, too."

But he didn't go to Tico until the doors were hung, the windows finished, and the roof bright with big thick shakes. The cabin smelled new, clean, tangy like the forest. It was large inside, one huge room with an earthen floor Shan intended to plank over later on. It looked long and low and everlasting. There was an opening for a stove-pipe, one of the things he would go to Tico to buy.

The barn wasn't finished but it was far enough along to shelter animals, something else he meant to buy. What he could have gotten along without was a genuine bed with springs and a ticking-mattress, but he knew he'd get those, also. And a wagon, a used one of course, and, if he could eke it out, maybe a driving rig, but that was pure luxury.

He would work over the list in his room at Otto's until the lamp wick smoked, then he'd go to bed and picture himself driving to Tico with a big black hat on the back of his head like Wyoming men wore, and perhaps smoking a cigar while the spring sun beat thinly across his big shoulders.

Over toward the foothills where the road was scored with tire gouges from those winter trips with Otto, over where the rim of the world looked close in the fresh clean air, would be Sarahlee at her cabin, in something that fitted tightly and showed her off. Dark eyes soft, strong arms bare, maybe her trim ankles showing—and, of course, a decent girl wouldn't do it—but maybe just a little of her legs showing, rounded and muscular and beautiful. He would sleep on that.

Then one day it became unusually warm. At breakfast Otto said it was a Chinook. The snow would melt, the earth would show through, black, marshy, swollen with rivulets.

"When will spring come," Shan asked. "After that?"

"After the Chinook, yes."

"Good. Then I'd better get to town and get the stuff for my cabin."

Mrs. Muller said from the background: "Do you have enough money, Shan?"

"I've got some," Shan said, arising from the table.

Otto looked at his wife. "He's got enough for now," he said.

"For cattle, for a team . . . ?"

"We got that worked out," Otto said, moving toward the door. His wife was wiping her hands. They exchanged a look, and she resumed her work.

Outside, it was forty above, pretty warm. Shan waited for Otto. "What'd you mean we got that worked out?"

"I've been meaning to mention it," Otto said as they walked toward the barn. "I got a hundred and eighty springing heifers. They'll calve-out this summer. Now then, first calf heifers need watching. You've picked that much up around here this winter. The first time they calve anything can happen . . . you can't just turn 'em out on the range and let 'em go. Calves get hung up, the heifers get scairt, do crazy things like abandoning their calves. I'm going to make you a proportion. You take them until they're calved out, watch them close, and I'll give you two-thirds of the calf crop. You'll get a start that way and you'll also be doing me a big favor."

Shan looked doubtful. "That's no favor," he said, "that's charity."

Otto shook his head adamantly. "If you knew this business like I do," he said, "you wouldn't say that, Shan. You'll be riding every day all day after they start calving. Some of the calves'll be hung up. You'll have to deliver them. I'll show you about that. No, Shan, if you think that's charity, go ask a cowman. He'll tell you I'm taking advantage of you. Out of the hundred and eighty heifers you'll get maybe sixty, seventy calves. For that you'll spend all summer at hard work."

Shan watched the ground as they walked. Bad enough to know nothing about cattle, worse to suspect Otto was fathering him, giving him charity.

Inside the barn Otto handed him a folded paper. "Give this to the man at the store," he said. "Say I'll be along next week to pick it all up with the wagon."

Shan pocketed the list, saddled up, and mounted the livery horse. Otto stood at his stirrup.

"You going to get some work clothes?" he asked.

The blue uniform was patched and stained. "Yes, see you later, Otto. I expect this'll take all day."

"No hurry. Bed down at the livery barn if it's too late," Otto said, and stood in the yard, watching Shan ride away. When he was small in the distance, Otto walked back to the house.

"You know what I think?" he said to his wife. "I think Shan's got women on his mind."

"He never said anything. . . ."

"Not around here, no. I don't think he even knew he was making woman talk around me." Otto shrugged, dropped his hands. "He's young. It's coming spring. . . ."

CHAPTER FOUR

He left Otto's list with the clerk of the General Mercantile Company at Tico and made several purchases of his own, then went across the road, paid the liveryman for the horse, and got involved in a complicated trade for a work team and the same saddle animal. The deal hinged upon whether the horse trader would credit the money paid him for use of the horse against the purchase of all three horses. This he agreed to do providing Shan bought a set of work harness from him, also. The way the wrangling ended was with Shan buying the team, the saddle horse, a set of used chain harness, and a saddle. The trader agreed to keep and feed the animals until Shan was ready to start back. Shan then took one of his bundles from the store into the liveryman's saddle room and shed his uniform, donned the conventional range wear, and emerged, self-conscious but satisfied, to inquire about the Gordon place.

He ate buffalo hump hash at a beanery then

struck out. The Gordon place was beyond town, and when he left the plank walk, mud accumulated with stubborn persistence upon his new boots. As he walked, he studied his list for the hundredth time, scowled in concentration, and estimated how far his money was going to go toward getting all he wanted. From time to time he had to stop and kick off the heavy adhering snowshoes of mud. Just before he got to the cabin, he bent, used his clasp knife to scrape the boots clean. When he straightened up and gazed at the cabin, a solid lump lay somewhere behind his belt.

When he knuckled the door, he half expected a hollow echo or a strange face. Instead, Sarahlee appeared as if by magic, exactly as he remembered her, and her eyes stayed on his face with a warm small smile.

"Shan, come in."

Inside, it was warm and there was a wonderful odor of boiling meat. The early winter gloom was thicker indoors. She moved around a table, worked at lighting the lamp there, and words flowed back to him. He didn't hear them. Bent over like she was, profiled, he studied her. When the light grew, it got tangled in her chestnut hair, made a deep, golden scar of the V in her throat. Her arms up high were half as large as his own arms, round and solid-appearing. She straightened up, still smiling and looking directly at him. The light made dusk lie in far corners in a room that was cozy and warmly personal.

". . . wondered about you. I even asked around town if anyone had heard of you. Only the liveryman knew anything, and that wasn't much."

"I have the cabin," he said finally. "I mean Otto Muller and I built it."

"Otto Muller?"

"He and his wife have that two-storied house way out there all by itself."

The cloudiness left her eyes. "Oh, yes," she said in quick recollection. "South of the Blessings'. I don't know them, though."

"Honest, plain folks," Shan said. "He knows that country like a book. I never saw a man who's as handy as Otto. He can build anything."

"I'm glad you didn't give up," she said.

"Give up? Why should I give up?"

She sat down on a shiny old leather sofa and motioned for him to sit, also. "The way you talked on the stage . . . about the cold. Remember?"

He sat down near her, but on the edge of the cushions. "That was just talk," he said, thinking she hadn't smiled at him like this on the stage, and without the coat her figure was smaller. He remembered the softness of her shoulder, the way she'd rubbed his hands. "You get used to this cold. I worked up there in shirt sleeves some days, and it didn't bother me at all."

"Is the land like you hoped? Will you make a ranch out of it?"

He loosened up after a while and talked, and she watched his head, the way it moved, how expressions emphasized what he said, and she noticed he used his hands more than he had before when he spoke. She also noticed how shaggy-headed he was. When the opportunity afforded she commented on it.

"You need a haircut."

He blinked at her. How long had it been? He ran his hand through the heavy growth and grinned. "I expect I do at that. I haven't thought much about haircuts."

She got up swiftly. "I'll do it for you if you'd like."

"You?"

"Certainly, you won't be the first, Shan."

"Well . . ."

"You sit there a moment and I'll be right back." She swept out of the room.

He leaned back and looked at the parlor. It had a layer of serenity, of silence and decorum the Muller place lacked. When she returned, she had a large white cloth, shears, comb, and even a small bottle of something fragrant.

"Sit on this straight-backed chair. That's it." She bent from behind him, swept the white cloth around, and for a fleeting second her hair brushed his face, her warmth radiated around

40

him. It became difficult for him to breathe.

"How large is the cabin?"

Shears snipped, locks of hair dropped away, and the combing made his skin tingle.

"Twenty feet wide and thirty-five feet long. Plenty big."

"That's almost too large, isn't it?" She turned his head with cool, strong fingers. "It'll take a lot of wood to keep it warm in winter."

"Well . . . I've got lots of trees up there. Besides, someday I may want it . . . that large."

Silence settled for a moment. The shears clicked, and she scooped up handfuls of hair on top, made long slices, then combed out what remained. For a while there was only the sound of the scissors, then she spoke again.

"Wyoming doesn't always make good first impressions. It can be raw at times."

He shrugged slightly. "Rawness isn't new to me."

"No," she said, "I know it isn't." For a second both hands rested on his shoulders; an aura of tenderness swept over him from those hands. Then she resumed her work briskly at the base of his head where short hairs stood straight out.

"What about livestock?"

"Well, Otto wants me to take a hundred and eighty first-calf heifers on shares. I don't know . . ."

"That's wonderful. That'll be your start, won't it?"

"It seems like charity to me. Otto says it isn't . . . but I've got a feeling like he's just doing it to help me out . . . get me started up there."

She swabbed hair from under the collar of his shirt. "It doesn't sound especially like charity, Shan. Isn't there a lot of work and responsibility to something like that?"

He told her, yes, there was, then repeated what Otto had said, and she finished the haircutting and combed his hair with gentle, long strokes. When he finished talking, she said: "It sounds like hard work, and if Mister Muller is like you say, then I'd certainly take his word about it."

"I guess I can help him in other ways, too," Shan said. "Branding, rounding up, haying, things like that."

"Yes, it sounds to me like he needs you as much as you need him." She moved around front, held up a small oval hand mirror. He looked into it and was surprised to see what a truly professional job she'd done. Where the hair no longer covered his flesh, it looked indecently white. She held out the comb and he dutifully took it but didn't use it. She had a twinkle in her dark eyes at his expression.

"You didn't think I could do it, did you?"

He looked at her and grinned. "I didn't know."

She put the mirror on the table, bent forward to unfasten the neck cloth, and he tried not to see the roundness of her flesh. He was perspiring. When she drew away, he got up, looked downward,

42

and brushed hair off his trousers and shirt. His tongue felt like a slab of frozen pine along the roof of his mouth.

"You bring the towel," she said, and started across the room. He followed her into a lean-to kitchen where the woodstove was hissing like it had green oak in the firebox. There was a simmering kettle over one burner and from it arose the tantalizing aroma he had smelled upon entering the house and it rekindled his appetite. Sarahlee had to tiptoe to put the shears and comb away on a high plank shelf. Shan stood there in the middle of the room, watching her. Her back was long from shoulder to hip, thicker on down but solid. She turned and took the towel from him, brushed back a heavy curl of her hair, and nodded toward the table. There were two places set.

"Now don't tell me you're not hungry," she said.

He looked at the two settings. "You're expecting company," he said.

She turned away, busied herself with the towel, and spoke over her shoulder. "No, I set that extra place when I came out to get the haircutting things."

"Well, I ate just before I came out here."

She turned around and was on the point of saying something when a loud knock sounded on the front door. He saw the quick look of apprehension darken her eyes before she moved past.

"Excuse me a minute."

He listened to her diminishing footfalls, then stood there feeling guilty about something vague in his mind, and awkward. Two voices made a blur of sound beyond the kitchen door. One was deep and strong, a man's voice. He went closer to the doorway, strained to hear, and when he could not, he peered around the casing. But Sarahlee's back was to him and the front door was only half open; he could not see who faced her beyond, out in the cold darkness.

He felt betrayed and closed the hands hanging at his sides. Then the man's voice became insistent and louder and dumb wrath began to pool in Shan without reason. He began moving without any notion of why, crossed to the door, pulled it out of Sarahlee's hand, and flung it wide open. The stranger in the dark turned a blank, astonished look upon him, but only for a second, then they recognized each other. It was the drunk, bearded man he'd met that first dawn in Tico— the man he'd knocked down in the saloon.

For several seconds no one said anything, then Sarahlee moved to close the door and block out the bearded man's face. She was upset.

"He didn't mean anything. It's just his way . . . to be hard to discourage."

Shan didn't know what to say so he said nothing. The sense of betrayal had spread all through him, made him feel almost ill. His imagination conjured up thoughts too vivid, too painful to tolerate. He went to the sofa, picked up his hat, and turned back toward the door.

"I better go. I'm not hungry anyway." He reached around her for the latch but she did not move out of his path. He lifted the latch, pulled inward, and a blast of cold night air touched them. "It's pretty late."

"Shan . . . don't go."

He spoke doggedly without looking at her. "I got a pretty big load of stuff to haul back. Better get some sleep so's I can get an early start."

She moved then, a breath of the night touched her hair, rustled it with the lamplight in it, made a golden chestnut sheen. "I'm glad you came by," she said, and her lips hardly moved at all.

"Thanks for the haircut."

"When it's grown out, I'll give you another one."

"Yes'm."

He walked away with his boot steps making a hard ring upon the frozen ground and he had never really hated anyone in his life—had never known anyone well enough to hate them—so now his feelings toward the bearded man were altogether new. They filled him to choking. He didn't think how it was—that a girl as handsome as Sarahlee Gordon couldn't go long unnoticed in a frontier village. All he knew was how painful those vivid imaginings were and by the time he got to the livery barn, where he meant to bed down, his eyes were as dead and dangerous as the thin ice beside the buildings.

The next morning he made a trade for a good used wagon, hitched the team to it, and went to the general mercantile, loaded up without speaking, and drove out of Tico with the saddle horse tied to the tailgate.

He drove all the way back to the Muller place without stopping. Without even making a cigarette or paying attention to the way his new team acted, or talking to himself, something he had grown to do of late when he was alone, dreaming out loud and savoring the sounds of his thoughts.

He saw Otto and Mrs. Muller come outside to watch the approaching wagon. It cheered him a little, knowing how large their eyes would be, how proud of his trades and his acquisitions. He hadn't told them all he had intended to buy in Tico. He saw Otto say something aside to his wife. She scuttled toward the house, and Otto headed for the barn where he was waiting when Shan drew up and looped the lines.

"My God, Shan . . . you even bought a bed!"

Shan climbed down. The bed had cost $18, but he wouldn't look at Otto because the dark mood had closed down upon him again. Shan went to the team, began unhitching them. Otto bent far over the wagon's sides, examining things, then at last he peered under the wagon, at its running gear, touched the iron tires for thickness and tightness, and walked up to study the horses. The team was good. Both horses were chestnuts, young and strong with straight backs and powerful shoulders. Otto followed Shan when he led them into the barn and put them in adjoining tie stalls and fed them. He followed Shan back outside when he went after the saddle horse.

"I had room," Shan said finally, "so I fetched back the things you had on the list. Save you a trip down, Otto."

They began unloading the Muller provisions, grunting as they moved them into the house, and into the stone pantry with sacks of flour, cans, and boxes. Mrs. Muller supervised the storing of articles with a minimum of talk. When it was all finished, Otto took the milk bucket back to the barn when they went to feed. He glowed from his labor, stopped by the wagon, piled still with Shan's things.

"Get that cannon cloth," he said to Shan, "we'd best cover what's still out here against the frost . . . and it might rain . . . it's rain-time of year."

After they'd covered the wagon, Otto jerked his head toward the loft. "Pitch down some hay while I milk." As Shan was climbing upward, Otto put his head to one side. "Didn't have any trouble in town, did you?"

"What kind of trouble? I didn't get into a fight, if that's what you mean." He disappeared overhead, and Otto watched him a moment before he sat down and began squeezing milk into the bucket with rhythmic sounds.

A moment later Shan appeared on the edge of the hay pile, looking down. "What made you ask that, Otto?"

"Well, not half hour after you left yesterday the Blessings rode by, headed for Tico."

"Well, hell," Shan said, "I don't even know them."

"No," Otto said slowly. "They stopped here for a while. They'd ridden past your cabin."

Shan leaned on the pitchfork. "You figured they'd look me up in town?"

"They said they were going to, Shan."

Shan turned away, began forking flakes of hay down into the mangers, and when he'd filled them all and worked his way back around to the ladder, he hung the fork up, descended, and leaned against the wall, watching Otto strip the cow dry.

"Maybe I left too early this morning."

Otto nodded. "Well, we knew they wouldn't like the idea of a cabin up there, Shan."

"Did you tell 'em it wasn't their land?"

Otto arose, hung the stool on a peg, and threw all his weight on one leg to offset the heft of the full bucket. "No," he said, "I didn't argue with them. All I said was that you owned that land and I'd helped you build that cabin and barn."

Shan started out through the door. "They must

not have wanted to fight very bad," he said carelessly, "or they'd have hunted me up yesterday."

Otto made no move toward the door. "I expect I had something to do with that," he said. "You see, I figured you were outnumbered . . . you don't know them even by sight and they're handy with guns to boot . . . and when they asked me to describe you to them, I said you were about my size and build with blond hair and spectacles."

Shan stared at Otto a moment, then he began to laugh. Otto shrugged and walked out of the barn. There was a hard twinkle in his eyes. "Let's go inside, Shan, I'm about half hungry."

As they neared the house, Shan said, "I bought the horse pistol and carbine, Otto. Even picked up a used shotgun. Got ammunition, too."

"Then you'd better start practicing. Use up all the shells you got if you have to. I'll pick up more when I go to town next time. Get real good with that pistol." At the doorway he turned. "I hate this," he said. "I hate to see trouble amongst neighbors out here."

"Maybe there won't be any. Maybe I can catch them without their guns some time and talk peace into them."

But Otto shook his head. "You'll never catch them unarmed, Shan, and there's something else you got to know, too. All this talk about gunfights . . . lies, Shan. The Blessings won't give you a chance. I've seen a hundred gunfights and I've known my share of gunfighters . . . I've yet to see either where someone didn't have an edge over the other fellow. A man that's good with his pistol baits a man who isn't, and kills him. What kind of sense does it make going up against a man who might be better than you are with a gun and who might kill you? None, none at all. The only man who ever wins against gunfighters is a wise man."

"Huh?"

Otto set the bucket down, hunched over, and peeked around the corner of the house as if at an imaginary enemy, cocked his finger, and tugged it back. "Like that," he said.

Shan's expression clouded over. He said nothing.

Inside, Mrs. Muller looked up at Shan, peered into his face, and said: "No fight?"

"I didn't meet them," he replied.

She smiled broadly at her husband. Shan saw the look they exchanged and dropped down at the table. "They'll figure what you did, Otto," he said. "You tricked them . . . they more'n likely won't like that."

Otto set out the whiskey crock and two glasses. "They don't scare me. One of us they might get, yes. *Both* of us . . . no."

But Shan wasn't as optimistic. They'd be nearly three miles apart. But he didn't mention it. Throughout supper he was mostly silent. When

Otto or his wife would say something, ask something, he would answer with a minimum of words. Otto looked at his wife and she looked back at him.

CHAPTER FIVE

The following day they took Shan's loaded wagon and horses up to the cabin. It was such a warm day that he and Otto were sweat-wet and dry-mouthed before they got the stove set up, the bed unloaded, the odds and ends hung on pegs or put upon the slab shelves. Mrs. Muller had come along for, as she'd said, you didn't just move into a new cabin, first you "warmed" it with a little celebration—a little party. She set them to cutting stove lengths at the wood pile, and there they really sweated. Shan finally removed his shirt and hung it on a little tree. Otto stopped, leaned on his axe, and gazed at Shan. After a while he wagged his head without speaking and went back to work.

When Mrs. Muller called them from the cabin, she pointed to the carefully erected washstand just outside the door. There was a thick and dazzlingly white towel hanging from the roller. Across its middle in dark yarn were Shan's initials. Otto laughed and made a mock bow permitting Shan first use.

They ate and worked until the shadows began to

lengthen, then Mrs. Muller said she and Otto had better leave. Shan stood in front of his cabin watching until they were lost to sight in the dusk, then he stoked up the fire, dug out a pipe he'd bought, whittled off some shag, got up a good head of smoke, and lay on the bed, smoking and thinking. At first it was peaceful, snug and warm and fragrant, and when a coyote howled, he listened, enjoying the melancholy sound. Then a specter came. At first it was vague, indistinct, then it got clearer and clearer until he recognized it, saw every pore in the gray skin, every straining muscle—a Rebel soldier who had hanged himself in a barn in Virginia. Shan had found him, cut him down. Who he was, why he'd hanged himself, Shan never knew. Now here he was again.

He relit the cold pipe and puffed it to life. The coyotes were closer, more numerous, when next they howled. He got off the bed, sought a book he'd bought, and sat down at the slab table, concentrating on the words, making them come off the printed page by sheer force, until he was exhausted, then he slept.

Three nights went by like that, with the coyotes and the memories. On the fourth night he heard the wailing howl of a wolf and its eeriness made him feel queer, as though he was detached from his body, from everything on earth and was far up in the moonlit night, looking down, seeing it all, himself included—those coyotes, that wolf, the night shadows of gaunt trees, the lift and roll of spun-out earth frozen into black immobility.

On the fifth day Sarahlee came riding up. He was in the unfinished barn when he heard the fluted sound of a distant yell. He stepped out into plain sight with his heart pounding and one hand upon the butt of the black pistol he wore. It took a while to recognize the rider, to separate the human outline from the horse's outline, to recognize the side-saddle, then he hurried across the yard to the wash basin, splashed water over his face and combed his hair, flung into the cabin for a fresh shirt, and was tucking it into his waistband when she came loping up.

There were faint drops of perspiration on her forehead. It was close to seventy degrees in the sunshine. She wore a little tight coat like artillerymen wore. It was very full. Her skirt was dark, sort of rusty-colored, and she carried her hat in one hand so that her hair shone like polished brass. She was smiling when she reined up, watching him in his doorway with uncertainty behind the smile. The horse fidgeted, acted nervous. He noticed how casually and confidently she handled it.

"When you said you wanted to be a hermit, you meant it," she said. "I thought I'd never get up here."

"What time did you leave town?" He couldn't think of anything else to say.

"Before sunup. Can I get down?"

He flushed and moved toward her. "Excuse me. You're pretty as a picture in that dress."

He helped her down, couldn't overcome the desire not to let go of her arm, so he held her with one hand and took the horse in the other, began leading them both toward the barn. There was a huge lump in his throat he tried to dissolve by swallowing. She filled her lungs with the clean air and let her lips lie apart while she looked far out.

"Two miles of it?"

"Two miles." He dropped her arm at the barn door, led the horse inside, fumbled at the cinch, the bridle, hung them awkwardly on a peg, and forked hay to the beast before joining her outside. Her cheeks were red, the darkness of her eyes full of luster. She turned slowly to look up at him.

"It's like you, up here. Big, rugged-looking." She smiled. "I love it. I always have loved it out here. When my uncle was alive and I used to visit him, we used to ride all over this country. He knew every cranny of it . . . he'd been a trapper and knew where every Indian battle took place." Her roving glance went to the cabin. "He'd have loved this, too. He'd have thought your cabin was wonderful. It's larger than I pictured it."

"Well, I told you how large it was."

"I can't envision distances. Most women can't."

"I'll show you how I've got it fixed up."

When they passed the door, the first thing he

saw was the dirty shirt on the floor near the bed. It looked five times its normal size. He picked it up, scarlet-faced, and stuffed it under a pillow, then showed her the stove, the cupboard he'd worked endless hours over, the shelf of books he'd bought —and hadn't completed reading even one of—and the towels Mrs. Muller had made with his initials darned into them. She touched things and smiled a lot, and when they were by the stove, she looked up at him.

"I could cook us supper before I go back."

"I'd sure like that. You know, learning to cook's not very easy." His courage was growing. He looked at her boldly. "You could teach me, I expect. A few trips up here and I'd learn."

She looked at the stove. "I'm all finished in Tico, Shan. Everything's done but getting the money for the cabin."

Silence descended, became a barrier between them. "Finished? You mean you're going back to Nebraska?"

"Tomorrow or the next day. Selling the cabin was all that kept me here this long."

He looked steadily at an improbably fat Morgan horse on a calendar they'd given him at the Tico Mercantile Company. "What a hell of a thing to say to me," he said.

She looked up swiftly, astonished.

He turned away. "Let's go outside," he said, "it's stuffy in here."

She walked just ahead of him with a puzzled expression. At the door she turned back. "What did you mean by that? Why was that an awful thing to say to you, Shan?"

He moved around her, out into the sun. "I don't know. I can't explain what I meant."

"Ryan . . . ?"

"Don't call me that," he said sharply. "I don't like that name. Stick to Shan."

She moved up close, gazed into his face, and whatever she saw made her look away.

"I'm sorry, Shan."

"There was a man at the orphanage where I grew up . . . he always called me Ryan, and the only time he called me was for a licking. In the Army when they read off your name . . . Ryan Shanley! . . . it means you've got to get ready for something. . . ."

She was looking at him strangely, her eyes round and still and very dark.

He raised a big arm suddenly, flung it out in front of him, and continued. The words were bitter and hating, like profanity. "See that flat out there, Sarahlee? Otto says that's where we'll cut hay this summer. Farther out . . . see where the lodgepole pines are? Those'll go into the rail fence I've got to build around the hayfield to keep the cattle out." The arm dropped. "The rest of it's all grazing land. Back East they'd plow it . . . out here you don't plow much." He frowned at the ground. "I've got to learn to make branding irons at Otto's forge. . . ."

"Shan."

He grunted dully and without looking at her. The sun was making the ground soft. There were tiny green things coming out of the black soil, small and countless, blades of grass as fine as hair.

"I'm happy for you."

"Maybe I put the cabin too far out."

"No, Shan. This is where it belongs. See . . . the mountains back there, the land falling away in front. I think it's perfect right here."

"Do you?"

"Yes." She was looking into his eyes. There was a strange hush in her expression.

"That's good," he said. "I was thinking of you when I put it here."

She didn't look away. Her gaze was fixed upon him. She drew in a big gulp of air and very solemnly she said: "Shan . . . I'm glad of that. I'm glad you were." Then she turned a little, facing slightly away from him. He could see the V in her throat and it was pumping erratically. "This is your world now, Shan. You belong here. That's what I meant about being happy for you. Whatever else has happened to you, wherever else you've been . . . Wyoming is home for you, your world, Shan."

"Our world, Sarahlee. You've always said how

you loved Wyoming. This here is for both of us, Sarahlee." He could see her mouth tremble. It upset him, and when next he spoke, he wasn't completely aware of what he was saying. "Hell . . . anywhere's my world . . . New York, Antietam, Wilderness, Richmond . . . here . . . it doesn't matter."

"Don't, Shan. You see I didn't understand. . . . I didn't know, exactly, Shan. Maybe I thought . . ." She turned and looked squarely at him. The pulse in her neck was slowing and her eyes were soft with a strong glow. "I think this is beautiful here. Wonderful. I adore the cabin. I like all of it, Shan." She watched the twitching muscle in his neck, knew how his fists were clenched. "Shan . . . I just didn't know . . . But that's all right. We'll make it all right." Her gaze blurred when she repeated it. "*We'll* make it all right."

"Marry me, Sarahlee? I've got to marry you."

She nodded, then it was as though something within her broke, crumbled. She hurried away from him, toward the cabin. She was crying.

When he bent over the bench by the washstand where she was sitting, she wiped her face and smiled up at him. "Don't look so . . . so . . . sick, Shan." She shook her head and perked up the corners of her mouth. "I like Ryan better, but I suppose I'll get used to Shan." Then she arose, leaned back against the cabin's wall. The sun hung in one place overhead. She turned after a moment and very slowly removed the artilleryman's jacket. The blinding whiteness of the blouse, its contours, sent blood pounding into his cheeks.

"This will be *our* piece of Wyoming," she said quietly, dropped the jacket upon the bench, and stood there looking beyond him, steeled against what was in his face. "All right, Shan."

He finally said—"We could eat some supper."—but food was the farthest thing from his mind.

"Let's just sit down," she said, and went back into the cabin where it was cooler. He only had one chair so he sat on the edge of the bed.

For a long time neither of them said anything, didn't even move, and happiness was a formidable pain inside him. He hadn't thought love would be hurting and now the old confusion came back. He opened and closed his fists, looked down at the ingrained dirt, the scars and scratches, and half-healed cuts—they were real, they were tangible. When he moved his fingers, he felt the pain from them. This other thing was intangible. It was fright and even a little dread. It reminded him of the first time a Johnny Reb had shot at him. The bullet he heard was real enough and he knew to duck from it, but he'd never seen it. Fear was something he'd never really understood anyway, and that day the Reb had shot at him he'd lain there on the ground, thinking about fear until an old infantry corporal with gray hair had sworn at him.

He still didn't understand it five years later, any more than he understood love. It wasn't altogether her white blouse, the dark richness of her hair, the bigness, the promise, the panting imaginings, it was putting his head on her shoulder, having her rub his hands; it was feeling the warmth of her gaze, seeing the encouragement of her smile; it was wanting to touch her and feeling ashamed for wanting to—it was pain.

She got up finally, moved to the stove, and said over her shoulder: "Wood for supper, Mister Rancher."

He went outside, brought back an armload, and dumped it into the woodbox. He stood behind her and watched the way she bent to build the fire, light it, and stand a moment in critical observation before she slammed the iron door. More than ever he was aware of her bigness. He was well over six feet tall and she was only a head shorter. She wasn't lean and stringy like most tall girls. She wasn't shriveled like the old woman. There was meat on her and it rippled when she moved, stood out when she strained. Then, for the first time, he noticed the fuzz on her cheeks. The sun slanted in just right to show that. He brought his arms up when she turned to set the graniteware coffee pot on a burner and held them uncertainly in mid-air.

She faced him and the serene calm was not there in her face. She didn't move back but neither did she go up against him, and when she spoke, it had nothing to do with a magic moment that flickered out with her first words.

"How do we do this, Shan? I've got to go back to Nebraska. My family just wouldn't understand it if I got married up here . . . just like this."

He lowered his arms heavily. "Well, we could get married in Tico, then you could go home, tell them, and come back, couldn't you?"

Her answer was delayed. When she looked up quickly, he burned brick red. She started to turn away, stopped, looked at the floor a moment, then turned back fully toward him, still with her head lowered. "I could do it that way," she said in a faint voice. He touched her. She drew up, raised her arms, and caught his head, drew it down until it was pressed against her bosom. He was shaking. "All right, Shan," she said in a soothing way. "We'll do it like you want to."

She didn't kiss him and he didn't notice it. The echoing thunder of her heart lingered long after he'd straightened up. "I'll go saddle the horses," he said. "We can stop with the Mullers for tonight."

"But what about the supper, Shan?"

"I couldn't eat now, Sarahlee. Honest I couldn't."

"All right. I'll bring you a cup of this coffee when it's hot."

She turned back toward the stove, and he went out into the sunlight where shadows were lengthening, growing thin and knife-like. Day was fast dying, but the heat lingered. By the time he'd saddled their horses, tied them outside the cabin, Sarahlee had his coffee ready. He drank in silence, put the cup aside, and helped her mount. It was pleasantly warm as they rode toward the road and down it. He reined over enough so that their legs touched once in a while. Once she reached up gently and touched his face like a mother would do to a small son. There was tenderness in her expression, deeply etched understanding, almost a sadness.

CHAPTER SIX

The Mullers were thunderstruck at what Shan told them. Otto opened and closed his mouth several times and never did get a word out, went to the kitchen table, and sat down heavily. Mrs. Muller was the first to recover. She seemed more excited than shocked, was more talkative than Shan had ever before seen her, and, when Otto made no move to do so, went herself to the under-stair closet and brought back the whiskey jug, set out two glasses for Shan and her husband, and poured Sarahlee a thimble glass of blackberry wine she'd made herself.

Otto gradually brightened. He drank a glass of whiskey though, before he finally found words.

"I didn't know you had a girl," he said, and studied Sarahlee with glaring approval. "Shan . . . you are a rascal. All this time you had a girl. . . ."

The kitchen glowed with mellowness and warm good feeling. Sarahlee and Mrs. Muller made supper. Mrs. Muller talked incessantly. Otto and Shan drank more whiskey, and when it grew late, Mrs. Muller took Sarahlee to the guest bedroom. That time Sarahlee kissed Shan. For moments afterward he sat stiffly in his chair, staring at the glass in his hand. Otto made no comment. After a while they began talking again. Shan nodded without hearing half what Otto was saying about the coming season for working the cattle, haying, finishing Shan's barn.

"We'll go to Tico in the morning," Shan said without any preface.

"Sure."

"She liked the ranch, Otto."

"That's good, Shan. But something else you got to learn, Shan. Women get lonesome in country like this. For us it ain't so bad, we got plenty work to do, but for women . . ."

"She can ride down here and visit if she gets lonely, Otto. I'll get her a nice top buggy, then she can drive down."

"That'll be good," Otto said. "But, Shan, we're older. Young people need young friends."

"The country'll grow, Otto. Someday there'll be other folks up here."

"I expect there will. Anyway, it'll all work out."

"Why shouldn't it?" Shan asked, big knuckles white around the empty glass.

"It will," Otto said soothingly. "All *good* marriages work out, Shan. A good marriage can work out anything. I just worry too much."

"I made that ranch for a purpose, Otto. I got that cabin for a purpose, too. To live in. To have a woman in. To maybe someday raise kids in."

"All right, Shan."

"No, not all right. I got this much coming to me from life, Otto. I never felt sorry for myself. I've managed to keep my gut full, to stay alive, but life's got to mean more'n that, Otto. Other men get wives, cabins, kids. I can have them, too." He pushed the glass away violently and stood up, big and flush-faced, breath pumping in and out of him audibly, in shallow bursts. "To hell with this," he said, "I'm going to bed." He turned, lurched, caught himself, and staggered out of the room.

Otto's eyes followed the big body. He listened to his sturdy house creak under Shan's large feet. He poured himself another shot of whiskey and looked at its amber color through the sticky glass, wondered at some of the other things Shan had said, and shook his head over them. A man ought to want more than a mother when he got a built-up girl like that. He drank the whiskey, struggled up out of the chair, and looked at Shan's empty glass. They must not have eaten up there, otherwise that whiskey wouldn't have knocked Shan out like it did.

"Bar the door, Otto," his wife called softly.

He barred the door and blew out the lamp chimney. The room got dark. Through the window the big, pale moon etched filigreed patterns upon the house through budding tree limbs, mottled the kitchen with splashed shadows. Otto tried to fathom the mood that was upon him and couldn't. He looked out the window for a long time.

"Otto . . . ?"

He crossed through the parlor to their bedroom. His wife was already under the covers, the lamp was turned down low. Otto began divesting himself of outer garments.

From the bed his wife said: "She's a pretty girl . . . big and strong, too."

He went on undressing, sat down to tug off his boots.

"What's the matter with you, Otto?"

"I don't know. Just a feeling about things is all."

"You don't think he should get married. It's their business, Otto."

"I know it's their business. I didn't say anything against it." He rolled back the quilts and climbed in. The bed groaned, sank down on his side. "Maybe it was too sudden. Maybe it isn't even their marriage. I don't know. Maybe it's this weather. I don't like to see it get so hot in April. By July it'll be a hundred and ten . . . no feed, no water, poor hay crop . . . a drought year if it keeps up this way."

"Do you know what she asked me? If we'd go down to Tico with them tomorrow and stand up for them at their wedding."

He gazed steadily at the ceiling a moment. "What'd you say?"

"That we'd *want* to stand up for them. She said she wished they could have a better marriage but Shan doesn't want to wait."

"No," Otto said, still looking at the ceiling, "I don't expect he does."

"There's nothing can't be put off another day."

"No."

"Good night, Otto."

"Good night."

He listened to his wife roll over on her side and burrow down under the covers and for a long time he couldn't sleep. When he finally dropped off, it seemed he'd only been asleep a moment when his wife was shaking his arm. Dawn was streaking the sky. He got up, dressed, took his coat and the milk bucket, and went outside. The new day was cloudless. A turquoise sky hung with narrow streamers of pink light greeted him. He put on the coat and trudged to the barn. Inside, animals bawled and nickered. He climbed to the loft, forked hay, and climbed back down, got the stool, drove the cow up, and hunkered down. The barn was warm and pleasant-smelling.

Shan loomed in the doorway. He had shaved and combed his heavy shock of hair. He blinked down at Otto. " 'Morning."

" 'Morning, Shan."

"Otto . . . I got a little drunk last night. I didn't mean to get roiled up in the kitchen like I did."

"You didn't say anything wrong."

Shan looked relieved. "I thought I might have." He moved deeper into the barn, looked at the eating horses. "Kind of worried me when I woke up this morning. You've already fed?"

"Yes. Shan, did you eat anything up at your place before you rode down here yesterday?"

"No," Shan said, leaning against the wall, "I didn't. Couldn't have if someone'd tried to make me eat with a pistol."

Otto looked at the milking bucket between his legs, gave an extra savage squirt into it. "It'll hit you that way sometimes," he said.

"That's what did it to me, I expect. Are you sure I didn't make anyone mad at me last night?"

"You didn't," Otto said, gazing up into the earnest, open face. "You sure got a guilty conscience, though. I know what you think you might have said but you didn't hurt my feelings or Georgia's, or Sarahlee's." He got up with the bucket, hung up the stool, and went out through the doorway. "Come on, let's go eat."

When they were almost to the house, Shan said:

"Sarahlee wanted you folks to come down to Tico with us, Otto."

"Sure, we planned to. I wouldn't miss this for the world, Shan."

Breakfast was gay but no one ate much. Sarahlee looked radiant to Shan. He didn't see the nervousness, the indecision. Mrs. Muller laughed a lot and even Otto seemed snared into the spirit of things and so they neglected to notice the large, lemon-yellow sun that hung majestically overhead and spilled heat down over the world, molten gold.

Mrs. Muller and Sarahlee did the dishes while Shan and Otto hitched the team to the wagon, drove down to the house, and sat there, waiting. Then Otto noticed the warmth, the cloudless sky.

"It's never been this warm in April before," he said.

"Early spring," Shan said, watching the house.

"I hope that's all it is."

Shan moved on the seat, then began to climb down. Otto watched him. "They'll be along," he said. "Women take longer to do anything than men could afford to take time for. Be patient."

When they finally came out of the house, Shan sought Sarahlee's eyes, held them with his own. She smiled. After he'd handed them both up and resumed his own seat, Otto lifted the lines, flicked them, and the horses leaned into their collars.

The road was dark and mushy-looking. New

grass was showing everywhere, like silk, green but too weak to do livestock much good yet. There were birds, too, and Shan thought it the most beautiful day he'd ever ridden through. He twisted on the seat to look at Sarahlee.

"You're going to love it up here," he said.

Her eyes twinkled at him. "How do you know? You've never seen a summer in Wyoming."

He laughed and Mrs. Muller turned on the seat to look at them. Otto began rummaging through his pockets for his pipe. He stoked it one-handed, lit it, and smoked hunched over, eyes fixed on something far off between the horse's ears. He said nothing.

CHAPTER SEVEN

They were nearing Tico before Shan shed his coat. Sarahlee had unbuttoned the little artilleryman's jacket. Otto straightened up a little, grunted, and pointed. Off to their left in the middle distance two horsemen were loping northward.

"The Blessings."

Shan strained to see. As he watched, one rider drew up. A second later his companion also stopped. They sat motionlessly watching the wagon go past. Shan tried to make out their features but the distance was too vast. Something about one of them was familiar. He would have dwelt on it further to himself but Sarahlee interrupted him.

"Who did Mister Muller say they were . . . I didn't hear?"

"The Blessing brothers. I've never met them. They own a ranch over the hill from our place a ways. Otto knows them."

"The most troublesome twosome in these parts," Otto said. "I get along with them all right . . . have up to now . . . but they're no good."

Neither man looked away from the distant riders so failed to observe a peculiar whiteness around Sarahlee's mouth. When the riders were far behind, Shan reached back and touched her arm.

"They don't mean anything to us, Sarahlee. Today I've got no worries anyway."

She smiled into his face, and Otto removed his pipe and pointed with it. "There's town. Haven't seen it since last summer."

His wife poked him in the ribs. "You thought maybe it wouldn't still be there?"

Otto smiled a trifle ruefully. "When you and I were married, the town was a little larger, but we didn't have as much to go home to as *they* have."

Mrs. Muller said to Sarahlee: "Otto was a wheelwright. His father was once a wheelwright in Germany. For you two, it's going to be better and I'm glad for that. We had hard times for many years, then we came out here. Here we've worked and saved. It will be like that for you two, work and save."

Sarahlee leaned forward and touched Shan's shoulder. She was squinting into the distance. "See my uncle's cabin from here?"

He found it with no effort and nodded. "Who bought it?"

"A miner named Callahan. He's new to Wyoming, also."

He looked around at her. "Also? I'm not new, not any more. When we get in, I'm going to buy me a wedding present . . . one of those big black hats Wyoming men wear."

"No, you're not supposed to buy your own wedding present. I'll buy it for you."

"All right. I already know what your wedding present's going to be. I almost bought it when I came down here after the other things."

"What is it?"

He faced forward as the wagon swerved. "You'll see." He got down to tie the team when Otto drew up.

The rest of it was like a half dream, half nightmare. They were married by a justice of the peace with a great golden watch chain dangling across his belly. The Mullers stood unnaturally straight and Shan never once looked the minister in the eyes. When they were back outside, Shan drew in a big breath and let it out. Tico looked different; the sun seemed hotter. In fact, Wyoming didn't

71

seem the same as it had before he'd gone into that house less than an hour before. Otto nudged him.

"What kind of a husband you going to make anyway? You were supposed to kiss her back there."

Sarahlee seemed smaller to Shan. She was standing beside Mrs. Muller. Now she laughed nervously, and Mrs. Muller put an arm around her. "Not out here in the road," she said sternly to Otto. "Go with him and get her present . . . go on."

"All right," Shan said, "where will you two be?"

"At the Mercantile."

Shan watched them walk down the plank walk. He momentarily forgot Otto who said: "Pretty as a picture." Then he laughed. "Today even my wife looks good."

They crossed the road together, and Shan led the way down an alley behind the livery barn, out into a yard where a row of buggies stood.

"That one, Otto. The top buggy with the yellow wheels."

Otto went closer. The buggy was used and dusty, but he could find no flaws in it. He tried to wobble the wheels; they were tight. He worried the tires, but they had no give. He put his weight on the iron step and hopped up and down several times, then he walked completely around it and finally got down to peer underneath at the running gear.

"How much, Shan?"

"Twenty-two dollars."

"Offer fifteen, go up to eighteen-fifty, and don't budge from there." Otto brushed off his knees. "You'll need a driving horse."

"I know. He had some pretty nice ones when I was down here before."

"Go see what you can do on the buggy, and I'll go around to the corrals and see what he's got." Otto walked away.

Shan entered the barn from the back alley. The trader greeted him with a wide smile. They began to trade. It required a half hour to barter for the top buggy at $19, then Shan and the trader went out back to the corrals. Otto nodded to them and pointed out an animal. This time the trading took even longer for Shan insisted on a set of driving harness being thrown in. By the time the trader had Shan's money, and he and Otto had the horse between the shafts, the morning was spent. Otto climbed in and sat back while Shan drove. When they tied up at the Mercantile, Otto got down and stomped mud off one boot. Shan came around beside him and they entered the store together. An odor of mothballs and oiled floors arose around them. A clerk came up. Otto pointed to a handsome black Stetson hat with a wide brim. "One to fit him," he said, indicating Shan. While Shan was trying one on, Mrs. Muller and Sarahlee came up. Shan smiled broadly at Sarahlee. The hat's darkness made his teeth stand out startlingly white. Otto paid for the hat and winked at his wife.

Shan led them outside where the buggy stood in sparkling sunlight. Mrs. Muller was stunned at Shan's extravagance and shot her husband a reproving glance. Sarahlee drew Shan's arm close and squeezed it.

"It's beautiful, Shan, simply beautiful."

"Something for you to drive when you go down to the Mullers'," he said.

"Darling, it's wonderful."

They went to the Clark House dining room for dinner, and Shan's ecstasy began to fade almost at once. Otto said: "Did you two find out when the stage's due?"

Sarahlee looked up swiftly, saw Shan's stricken look, and bit down hard on her lip. Mrs. Muller nodded at her husband. "Well," Otto demanded. "How much time we got?"

"Not very much," his wife said. "Half an hour."

Otto ate a good meal but Shan only picked at his food. Sarahlee ordered only coffee. Mrs. Muller ate a piece of pie. When Otto looked at his watch, they all arose, left the hotel, and trudged across the road to the stage station, and there they stood around, awkwardly waiting.

Mrs. Muller hugged Sarahlee. Otto got his pipe going and seemed drowned in the peculiar gloom that had been bothering him since the evening before. He roused only when Sarahlee said good bye, standing close and looking straight into his eyes.

"Take care of him, Mister Muller."

"Yes," Otto said, "we'll take care of him. You get back as soon as you can."

"Don't worry about him," Mrs. Muller said to the girl. Her eyes were damp. "Don't worry about anything. He's like a son to us, so don't worry about him. We'll watch things. I want you to come right back, Sarahlee . . . right back."

"I will. No, I won't worry about him, Missus Muller." She turned quickly away from the older woman. "Shan . . . ?"

He was standing there and for some reason his legs ached. The pain was back behind his belt, too. He wanted to reach out and touch her face, her shoulders, but he couldn't, so he took her hands and held them and looked lost. She kissed her fingers and touched them against his mouth. He didn't kiss them back, but what he felt was frank and open in his eyes and she understood.

"Ten days, Sarahlee?"

"Shan darling," she said quietly, firmly, "three weeks at the least . . . you know that."

He bent forward impulsively and whispered in her ear. "Christ, Sarahlee . . . waiting's going to drive me crazy."

She looked straight ahead for a moment, then drew his head down. "Don't say things like that,

Shan, it's blasphemy. Now be good and write to me and I'll answer you. Good bye."

The three stood together and watched her board the stage in silence, and remained like that, a forlorn little group, until the coach swung wide around a far corner and disappeared easterly. Then Mrs. Muller touched her face with a handkerchief and Otto cleared his throat, knocked out the pipe that had gone cold, and said: "We'd better start back. It's going to get dark before long."

Shan's buggy mare followed the Muller wagon out of Tico northward. He held the light lines in a listless hand and watched the off-center moon climb skyward. The roll of land slid rearward unnoticed and for once he didn't even hear the coyotes.

When they got to the Muller place, put up the animals and went inside, Mrs. Muller made a meal for the three of them. It was a dolorous affair and each of them was glad when it was over so they could go to bed with their private thoughts, be alone in the private world of darkness and silence.

Otto hadn't brought out the jug and Shan had been glad that he hadn't. He lay there in the hush, feeling hot and more lonely than he'd ever felt in his life.

CHAPTER EIGHT

When Shan found Otto the following morning, he was standing in the barn doorway, looking up. There wasn't a blemish in the sky; it was immaculately cloudless.

"It's supposed to rain this time of year," Otto said reproachfully.

Shan moved past, hooked hold of the loft ladder, and began the climb upward. "It will," he said. "If not today or tomorrow, then later." He forked down feed and didn't hear Otto.

"Later may be damned well too late."

Shan climbed back down, walked around the buggy mare, and patted her, then hunkered down near where Otto was milking. Beyond the doorway the yard was green, balmy, and sunlit. Mica in the earth shone like diamonds. He thought it was beautiful in spite of the soft ache inside him.

"Can't afford a drought this year," Otto said.

Shan was heeding nothing but missing Sarahlee. "Don't worry, Otto, it'll rain."

Otto frowned down at the bucket and said no more. They went in to breakfast together as usual, but after the meal Shan hitched the mare to the buggy and headed for his ranch, letting the mare pick her own way and gait. Once he thought of what Otto had said and looked skyward, found nothing there but more beauty, lowered his gaze, and watched the land unfold on both sides of the rig. His thoughts went back to an image of Sarahlee, drawn by a magnet that was passion and longing, subtle, indefinable longing.

A half mile beyond the witness tree he smelled something burning. For several hundred yards he sniffed without comprehending, then something took hold of his heart and squeezed. He stood up and peered from under the buggy's tasseled top but there was no smoke. He flicked the lines at the mare. She broke over into a nervous little trot, catching some of his uneasiness.

Then he saw it. His barn was in ruins. There was extruding blackness and char where it had been, little wisps of soiled smoke curling upward in the sparkling air. He roared an oath and lashed at the mare. She gave a mighty leap. He was flung off balance and fell back upon the seat, struggled to his feet, and lashed her again until the buggy was careening wildly, wheels spinning into solid silhouettes.

When he was closer, he saw three horses standing listlessly in his yard near the cabin. One had a saddle on its back with brass tacks studded into it. Shan drew and cocked his revolver. He was driving the rig like it was a chariot, standing up, the lines in one hand.

He swirled easterly in a slewing cloud of dust. Up ahead someone let out a yell. He saw two of them run out into the open away from his cabin. Both had carbines in their hands. At that distance all he could do was make out that they were men. Bending his knees to absorb the movement and vibration, he leveled his handgun and fired. One of the figures bounded into the air and lit, running. Another one ran up from nowhere and kneeled. Shan was hauling back hard on the lines when that one fired. The bullet didn't come close. He catapulted out of the buggy and shot once, standing still. The kneeling man fell sideways. From around in back of the cabin a figure emerged on horseback, bent far forward and riding hard. Shan fired and missed. The third figure also fled.

When the first rider burst into sight again, he was far over one side of his mount, the sun shining off his carbine held beneath his horse's neck. For some reason he did not return Shan's fire. He was very quickly out of pistol range.

Shan trotted forward with his gun dangling and his throat parched and feeling tight. He toed the crumpled figure over onto its back. It was a young buck Indian. Shan's bullet had struck within two inches of the dead man's heart, to the right a little. Standing there with sweat dripping from his chin, running down between his shoulder blades under his shirt, he heard the same cry again. It galvanized him to life. He ran to the cabin, pushed aside the door, noticed fleetingly how it had been forced, the hasp broken, found his carbine behind the stove, and hurried back outside. The dead Indian's horse was tied under a scrub oak tree. He leaped upon it, jerked it around, and used the carbine butt to get speed.

The animal was large and fast. There was a small US branded along its neck. It responded to Shan's urgings with every sinew. The wind whipping past drove water from the corners of its rider's eyes but even so he was forced to ride a full two miles before he saw the two Indians.

They were watching him, sitting their horses close together. It took a moment for the enraged white man to comprehend; they thought he was their companion. He bent low to simulate a hard-riding buck Indian until he was close enough, then he slammed the big gelding back on its haunches, slid off, dropped to one knee, and fired the carbine. The foremost Indian threw up his hands and went backward off his horse. The surviving hostile turned to flee without making any attempt to shoot back.

Shan remounted the cavalry horse and pounded it forward again. It was almost immediately evident his horse was far stronger than the one ahead, that he would overtake the escaping Indian. Twice he threw the carbine up and twice he lowered it. The muzzle jerked too erratically to fire; there was slight chance of hitting the fleeing Indian while he was in motion.

Seeing the inevitable fast approaching over his

shoulder, the remaining Indian yawed wide and made desperately for some trees. He was very close to them when Shan hauled back, set his mount in an earth-spewing slide and rolled off him. He kneeled to aim, and the Indian swerved again just as he fired. He levered up another cartridge, fired, and watched the horse and rider go down in a wild tumble. The Indian's gun flew out of his grasp, spun far out ahead of the crumpled horse. The Indian struck hard, didn't move.

Shan stood up slowly, reloaded, grabbed the single rein of the war bridle on the cavalry horse, and began to walk forward. His anger was burned out. He was panting with exertion and wringing wet with sweat. By the time he was standing over the Indian a muscle in his neck was quivering.

It wasn't a fighting buck; it was a young, inert squaw with a trickle of dark blood at one corner of her mouth. Perfectly straight, black, downward lashes hid her eyes. She wasn't more than sixteen, seventeen years old. Her hairline was low, the hair swept severely back. It lay raven-black, shiny, around her shoulders. Her dress was chalk-white, heavily ornamented with beadwork, quill-work, and graceful fringe. One leg was exposed and it shocked Shan to see how much whiter it was above the knee than below. He moved his foot, used the boot to push the dress down. The sun was hot on his bare neck, hotter through the cloth over his shoulders and down his back. He felt terribly thirsty.

Bending, he leaned over the carbine. Finally he reached down and pulled her around so that she was facing upward. She wasn't tall or heavily made; her body was compact, breasts the size of crab apples, fingers long and tapered. He thought she didn't look like any Indian he had ever seen, and when she opened her eyes, he watched them widen, flood with fright at sight of his red, large face so close to hers. She didn't move or make a sound.

He took a crumpled bandanna from a pocket, reached over without meeting her stare and daubed away the blood on her mouth. It was a pretty mouth. She might have lain like that an indefinite time, staring upward without moving, gripped with terror like a wild animal, but his legs began to ache from bending over the carbine so he took her by the arm and pulled her up. She was more than a foot smaller than he was. She made no attempt to turn away, to run, to fight. He held the carbine loosely in the crook of his arm, looked at her, and finally spoke.

"Who are you? Why did you burn my barn?"

She made no reply but he thought her dark glance showed a glint of understanding. The silence between them grew awkward. He drew the cavalry horse closer, motioned for her to mount. From the animal's back she stared down at him from eyes as black as obsidian and just as inscrutable. He returned the look until he felt uncomfortable, then turned and began to trudge along leading the horse. He stopped briefly to look at her dead mount. The bullet had pierced its chest from one side to the other. Farther on, he stopped by the dead buck. That bullet had caught the Indian full in the throat. Shan picked up the gun, cut the shank that kept the dead man's horse tethered to the corpse, and walked on leading both horses.

It grew still warmer. He finally took off his coat, handed it to the girl without speaking, and continued to lead both horses. He felt no desire to ride bareback any more. By the time they arrived back at his cabin, there were blue-tail flies walking over the first dead warrior. Shan systematically took the corpse's knife, hatchet, carbine, even his leather pants and fancy moccasins, then he caught the loose horse, took all three to the shade of a scrub oak thicket, tied them there, and got a spade. The young squaw sat by the wash-stand, watching every move he made. He ignored her, dug the grave five feet from the corpse, and when he was satisfied with its depth, used his boot toe to roll the body into it. He filled the hole, stamped it, with sweat streaming off him, put the spade against the front of the cabin, and got a dipper full of water.

Out a ways the buggy mare was grazing placidly

still harnessed to the rig. Having stripped to the waist for the digging, he now washed his upper body in cold water and felt new life flowing under his skin. Still ignoring the little squaw, he went past the broken door, got a fresh shirt, put it on, went back to the doorway, and gestured to the girl. When she was close, he pointed to the horse and buggy and started forward. She immediately fell in beside him and strode along without a sound. He growled at her after he'd caught the mare. She got up onto the seat beside him, and they drove to the barn.

The devastation sickened him all over again, but up close it was worse. His team had been tied inside. They smelled like roast beef. He stood around a long time just looking, kicking the curled hulk of his saddle, the tines of his handleless pitchfork, then he unhitched the mare, put her in a corral, and left her there. When he started back toward the cabin, the Indian girl followed him dutifully. He motioned her to walk beside him, not behind. By then his ferocity was ashes. The killings didn't enter his mind but remorse over the burned barn made him feel whipped, defeated, spiritually exhausted.

It was cool in the cabin. The girl went over by the stove and stood perfectly still. One side of her mouth was swelling, making her appear to be sneering at him.

"You red bitch, I ought to kill you."

She remained like stone, watching him. Beyond her, out through the door, he could see tendrils of wispy smoke rising, faint and burdened with the unpleasant odors. He sat down heavily at the table, all loose and limp, hands hanging like dead birds at his sides.

"Didn't get a chance to fire the cabin, did you?" He turned away from the ruin outside and stared at her. "I thought redskins stole horses not burned them." He saw the coffee pot where Sarahlee had left it. It alone stood as he remembered it; the rest of his possessions had been pawed over. He got up, picked up the switch broom, and held it out. "Here, clean this mess up, damn you."

He went out of the cabin, slammed the door, and stood in the dazzling sunlight unsure what he must do next.

"Ho! Shan!"

He was drawing the pistol when he turned. It was Otto. He was riding in a long lope, reins in one hand, his rifle in the other. He was bareheaded and sitting very erect in the saddle. Shan let the pistol drop back into its holster. Otto rode up, stopped, and sat there, staring at the barn. Shan made a fierce gesture.

"Indians! I came up just as they were plundering the cabin. I killed them." He pointed to fresh dark earth close by. "One's buried right there. Another one's out a ways." The arm dropped down limply. "Look at my barn. . . ."

Otto dismounted ponderously, squatted in the shade in front of his horse. "Well," he said resignedly, "I expect we got to build that one over again."

Shan dropped down beside him. "What's the use? What's the god-damn' use, Otto. Look at it. . . ."

"What kind of Indians, Shan?"

"Indians. Greasy-looking redskins. The last one . . . I shot her horse out from under her. I should have killed her, too."

"Her?"

Shan jerked his head toward the cabin. "In there. I thought it was a buck."

"You brought her back?" Otto asked, gazing steadily at Shan.

"Yes, I brought her back."

"Why?"

"Why?" Shan repeated slowly. "Well, she was knocked out when the horse went down. . . . I don't know . . . I just brought her back." He was silent a moment, then: "She can work it out. She can help Sarahlee work around the place. Look at that barn. If I hadn't come up when I did, they'd have burned the cabin, too."

Otto got up stiffly, massaged one knee. "Well, all right. We've got to rebuild it, only let's not put the next one in the same place. Bad enough to have the first one burned down without having to move all that rubbish to build another one."

"Otto, I can't ask that of you. I just plain can't."

"You've got to have a barn, boy. You've got to have a place to store hay, keep your horses." He looked down suddenly. "Where *are* your horses?"

"They burned the team. They were tied inside."

"That's what the smell is."

"I got two of their damned Indian horses."

"Any good?"

"I don't know. They're both big animals. One's branded **US** on the neck. He's well-broken."

"To saddle," Otto said. "Well, I expect we can break them to harness." He dusted his britches off, straightened up. "All right, Shan, I'll be over in the morning. We'll start snaking trees down here again. Sooner we get started the better. We don't have too much time. It'll be an early turn out this year." He mounted his horse, remembered something, and bent forward. "Go get the squaw, Shan. I want to see what kind of Indians they were."

Shan went to the cabin and threw open the door. She was down on her knees, examining something. She looked up swiftly, then leaped up, her movement reminding him of a wild animal, a small deer poised to run. He motioned her outside. She walked ahead of him, stopped dead still when she saw Otto staring down at her from the back of his horse, rifle across his lap.

"Southern Cheyenne," Otto said.

Shan looked down at the girl and shrugged.

She looked even smaller, younger now, than she had an hour before.

"You can tell by their clothes. You say there were two bucks with her? They must have been traveling through, probably going west to visit kinsmen at some Northern Cheyenne get-together. It'd have to be something like that or they wouldn't have a squaw along." Otto gazed steadily at the girl. "Can you talk English?" he asked.

The girl was mute.

Shan said: "She doesn't talk at all. Just stands still and stares at you."

"Did you hit her there in the mouth?"

"That happened when her horse went down. I was aiming low, for her body, the horse was running. I guess he was in the air when I shot because the slug went right through him."

Otto straightened in the saddle. "I'm not sure it's wise to keep her," he said. "If she's got folks, they'll come looking for her."

Shan looked down. "I'd like to see a few more," he said, then he looked up at Otto. "How would they know? The two bucks with her are dead. Who'd tell them what happened to her . . . where she is?"

"I expect that's right, too," Otto replied. "Didn't she fight you or try to run away?"

"No. I put her on a horse and brought her back here. All the time I was burying the buck in the yard here, she just stood there, watching me."

For the first time since riding up Otto looked amused. "You put her on a horse and led her back here . . . she riding and you walking?"

"I thought she was hurt," Shan said.

"That probably surprised her. Indians don't let squaws ride when they have to walk. They don't think it's manly to do that."

"I don't know anything about it," Shan said carelessly. "All I know is my barn's burned down and I'm starting a private graveyard for trouble-makers right here in my yard."

"Yeah," Otto grunted. "Well, we haven't had any serious Indian trouble around here in five years. They've been pushed farther west." He lifted the reins, turned his horse. "I guess there's nothing to worry about, Shan. I'll be back about dawn. We've got lots of work to do before your missus gets back."

Shan watched Otto lope to the road, swing southward, and disappear. He sent the girl back to clean the cabin, went over where the horses were, made hobbles, and turned them loose to graze. By then it was late afternoon, the sky was all speckled looking and red, each mark upon it like a horse's hoof. He poked around the barn rubble until it was too dark to see, then returned to the cabin. Inside it was as dark as a tomb. He could make out the Indian girl's silhouette over by the stove. Knowing she was watching him, he growled something inaudible, went to the table, and lit the lamp. She followed each movement with her eyes. Her face remained smoothly expressionless. He pointed to the stove.

"Make fire," he said. "Make something to eat."

But it was useless and he knew it. Even if she understood, which he doubted, she would not move so long as he was there to watch her, so he made supper, poured two cups of coffee, and dished up two plates of food, set them on the table with the implements, and motioned her forward. "Sit down," he said, enunciating with exaggerated clearness. "Eat!"

She sat down but did not eat. Her eyes followed every move he made. When he tilted the coffee cup back, their eyes met over its rim. He set the cup down hard.

"Damn you, quit that staring and eat!"

She ate. She bowed her head until lamplight showed blue-black in the hair of her temples, used her fingers instead of the spoon beside her plate, and ate. It dawned on Shan she did not know how one ate at a table.

He arose, filled his pipe with shag, lit it, got a pencil and some paper, and returned to the table, sat hunched over, and began a letter to Sarahlee. The only sound in the cabin was of the pencil pushing steadily across the page. He wrote of the burned barn, the Indians he'd killed, the captive Indian girl. He looked up. She was watching the pencil move over the paper, round-eyed, lips parted, hands barely visible over the rim of the table. He put the pencil down and gazed at her. The futility of speaking held him silent. What was she thinking? What did Indians think, anyway? Maybe he'd killed her husband. He unconsciously glanced at her fingers, then he smiled to himself. Where would she wear a wedding band—probably through her nose.

When she raised her face, looked into his eyes, she seemed intelligent, but how could you tell? He felt the vast gulf between them and frowned down at the half-finished letter. What difference did it make, wise or stupid, she was a squaw-Indian, about like a she-wolf, a mare horse, or a bitch dog. He went back to writing the letter.

When it was late, the letter finished, he made a pallet on the floor by the stove and told her by motions to lie down. She did, fully clothed and without once looking away from him. He reloaded his pipe and sat uneasily on the edge of the bed. Should he tie her? Would she cut his throat while he slept, shoot him—maybe take his scalp and ride away beating her breast or whatever squaws did when they avenged someone. He sucked on the pipe and frowned at the wall, then he got up, picked up the carbine, and unloaded it, put the cartridges in his pocket, and took his skinning and cutting knives from the shelf by the stove and laid them on the bed. After that he kicked his boots off and lay down, still wearing the pistol. When his pipe went out, he looked down at her but she was twisted away from him, face averted. He watched her for a while, then raised up on one elbow, blew down the lamp chimney, and plunged the cabin into darkness. Lying back with the comforting bulge of the pistol near his arm, he smiled grimly. She wouldn't cut his throat because he wouldn't go to sleep.

He thought of Sarahlee, of the burned barn, and of Otto—Otto. He wished he was like Otto. Steady, always knowing exactly what to do and how to do it. Coyotes howled outside. He turned his head and looked down. She was asleep. The little bitch wildcat was asleep just like she was at home—in her own teepee or hovel or whatever she lived in. He scratched his head, wiggled his toes, and sighed. When he fell asleep, he had no knowledge of doing it until he opened his eyes, moved them across the ceiling, then swiftly, in alarm, dropped them to the pallet. She wasn't there.

CHAPTER NINE

Shan swung off the bed, feeling for his gun, seeing the knives undisturbed, tugged his boots on, and looked in the corner where he kept the carbine. It hadn't been moved; beside it lay the Indian clothing he'd stripped from the dead buck.

He straightened up frowning, then it struck him— the horses!

He burst outside and halted with the new sun slanting downward into his eyes. There they were, out a ways, grazing, hopping from time to time with their hobbles. He turned away from the sun. Where was the squaw, then? He went back to the cabin door and quartered a little looking for sign, found it, small moccasin tracks in the churned dust. He was moving to track after them when he saw her. She'd been over to the spring and her hair was shiny with a high gloss. Her face, as smooth as ever, glistened from the cold water. She hesitated at sight of him, then walked past and into the cabin. He scratched his head again, but harder.

He washed and made breakfast, put it on two plates as he'd done the night before, and this time he did not have to tell her to eat. She used the spoon as though she'd secretly practiced with it. After breakfast, he hauled a bucket of water, set up the dishpan, and showed her how to wash the utensils. She plunged her arms into the water and soaked both sleeves. He swore at her, reached down, and yanked the sleeves up past her elbows. Her flesh was firm and warm, lighter where it had been protected from the sun. He stood, looking at her, but she did not look up. He was amazed at the smallness of her arms, at the slightness, the fineness of her bones, the milky texture of her skin. The creak and groan of a wagon roused him.

It would be Otto approaching. He took tools—an axe, several wedges, a hatchet, and a spade—and waited by the washstand beyond the door. Otto greeted him with a slow nod.

"Still got the squaw or'd she run off?"

"Still got her," Shan said, climbing into the wagon. "I taught her how to wash dishes, Otto. By the time Sarahlee gets back, she'll be a real help around the place."

"Maybe. I never liked having them around. Like a biting dog or a spoiled mule, work for you for ten years, then one day up and stick a knife through your guts."

"Aw," Shan scoffed, "she's too little."

Otto drove toward the distant forest without replying. For a week they did nothing but haul logs. After that they notched, peeled, adzed, and hoisted them into place. The squaw cooked for them, and two days in a row Mrs. Muller rode over with Otto. She showed the girl how to make simple things like hoecakes, fried meat, and boiled greens. She was interested in the girl, taught her ten words of common English, and told Shan he should teach her more, that she was very intelligent, but that she would be worthless to Sarahlee if she didn't know English. Shan said he would, and forgot about it. When he went to bed every night, he died with exhaustion. Only once did the little Indian come into his mind. That was the evening he went down behind the new barn to the spring box to take a bath. He was standing there, stark naked, moon glow glistening over his wet body, rubbing vigorously with the lye soap Mrs. Muller had brought over, when he turned and saw her standing in the dark gloom at the corner of the barn.

He was more chagrined than angry. "Get out of here!" he yelled, bent down, caught up a clod, and flung it. It struck over her head, powdered her hair with dust. "You red bitch, get out of here!" She faded into the night without a sound but Shan didn't forget and wouldn't look at her until near the end of the second week. When he told Otto, the older man laughed softly, then looked thoughtful, began watching the girl when Shan was around.

They were working on shakes for the roof. She brought them cold water like Mrs. Muller had taught her to do, set the bucket down, and said: "Gold watern."

It struck Shan as funny and he picked up the dipper and held it out. "Here, Otto, have some gold watern."

Otto smiled, drank, put the dipper back in the bucket, and looked up at the girl. "What's your name?" he asked.

She shook her head. Mrs. Muller had taught her to do that when she didn't understand. Otto kept gazing at her.

"She ought to have a name," he said, stopped

working. "I can't figure out why she hasn't run off, Shan."

"Why should she? She's got a roof, plenty to eat, doesn't have to work hard."

"Yes, but they aren't like us. Those things don't mean a lot to an Indian."

"Well, maybe she figures I didn't kill her when I should have, and she owes me something."

"It might be that," Otto said, reaching for the hatchet. He looked thoughtful. "Well, call her Jane or Mary. That's what we usually name filly colts when they're born . . . Christian names."

She became Mary.

Otto went to town the end of the third week. His wife wanted flour and Shan's blower needed new bellows so they could forge iron rings and tholes for the new barn, which was almost completed. It shone with newness, was richly fragrant of the forest, the running sap, and during the course of its construction they had broken Shan's Indian horses to harness. While Otto was gone, Shan whittled pegs and drove them into the mid baulk for harness and the saddle he was using—the one he'd gotten from the Indians and had pulled the gee-gaw tacks out of—and for the new pitchfork Otto would bring back from Tico.

It was a massive and beautiful barn to Shan. He walked through it, whistling, glowing with sweat and steely muscles. His flanks were lean from labor, his lungs stronger than ever.

When Otto returned, he had a letter from Sarahlee. It was soiled from much handling and limp. As soon as Shan got it, he sat down in the dust, rested his back against the barn, and read it. There were trodden weeds around him and a carpet of tall grass swept away as far as one could see in every direction. The time for haying wasn't far off.

Otto had brought Mrs. Muller back with him. They planned on spending the night at the cabin, taking Shan back with them in the morning to brand and mark the cattle.

High on the roof Otto nailed shakes, trimmed edges, put the finishing touches on, and every once in a while he'd look up at the sky with a critically anxious expression. When he was getting ready to descend, he glanced over the side and saw Shan holding the letter with both fists like it was trying to bite him. His head was bent in concentration and a big lock of dark hair hung low over his forehead. His lips were pursed as though in pain.

"What's it say?" Otto called down. "When's she coming back?"

Shan looked out around the paper at Otto who was coming down the ladder. "Her paw's sick. She doesn't know when she'll be back. Maybe next month."

Otto was holding the ladder with one hand. He shook his head. "Sorry to hear that," he said, looking straight at Shan. "Well, we got the barn finished . . . tell her that in the next letter, Shan." He moved closer in the hot sunlight, sank down against the barn, staring straight ahead. "A few more weeks. If it can't be helped, son, why I expect you don't want to get upset about it."

Shan ground the letter in one big fist. "The hell I don't," he said. "I got a wife and I haven't got a wife. I waited all my life . . . god dammit!"

Otto got up, dusted the seat of his pants. "Those weeks'll fly by, Shan, you'll see. We start working the cattle tomorrow. I figure that's going to take a full week. Then we've got to drive them 'way out on the range, and cut out those hundred and eighty heifers." He started to move toward the cabin. "Come on, Shan, let's eat. You're going to be surprised how fast those weeks'll go by."

Mrs. Muller's face grew long when Shan told her what Sarahlee had written. She and Mary fed them and there was very little talk. Afterward, Shan and Otto went out to hook up the wagon. They loaded the tools in it, and Otto said he thought Shan ought to drive his top buggy because there wasn't enough room in the wagon for all of them. Shan got the mare, harnessed her, and hooked her between the shafts. When Mrs. Muller and Mary came out, the girl went straight to the buggy and climbed in. Shan looked at her in displeasure for a moment, then raised his voice.

"Hey, Otto, why don't you ride with me, and the squaw can ride with Mrs. Muller?"

Otto climbed down. His wife leaned over and sharply said something to him. He hesitated, looking up at her, then trudged back to the buggy. Shan spoke the girl's name and gestured toward the wagon. She got down and went forward, climbed up beside Mrs. Muller and the wagon moved out.

Otto lit his little pipe and leaned back. "Shan," he said quietly, "Georgia says you shouldn't call her a squaw."

Shan looked at the trim, slight body high on the wagon seat far ahead and frowned. Otto was right. Now that she could understand some English, it probably wasn't nice to call her that, probably hurt her feelings, too, Shan thought, and he didn't want to do that, not after the way she'd pitched in without a word and worked as hard as any of them. He made no reply.

"It's all right with me," Otto went on, "only Georgia don't think you ought to."

"She's right," Shan said, and fell silent until they were well down the road toward Mullers', then he blew out a big breath and shook himself like a dog coming out of a creek. "I should've married an orphan like I am, Otto. There wouldn't be any paw to get sick then."

Otto spat and gazed at the sky. "Three weeks from now you'll wonder where the time went." He squinted his eyes. "If we don't get a rain pretty soon, we're going to have trouble this year."

Shan looked at the profusion of waving grass all around them. "Looks like we've got enough feed to me, Otto."

"*Now*, yes. We didn't get a drop of rain in April. This grass'll start to wither within another week or so . . . by July there won't be a blade left for the cattle to graze off. By August they'll be eating dust." Otto's pipe bubbled. "It keeps me awake nights, thinking about it."

Shan heard without heeding. He was thinking of Sarahlee, of the column of her neck, how that V in her throat plunged down into the white blouse under that little artilleryman's jacket, swelled, thrusting out. He was holding the lines so hard his fingers were sweat-slippery. The way light hung and shimmered in her hair. The way she looked distantly at him when he swore. How she looked when she laughed and the way she rode a horse, the bigness of her. *God, keep her for me. . . . Protect her like hell!*

Shan and Otto put up the horses while Mrs. Muller took Mary into the house. There were tools to put away, chores to do. By the time the men headed toward the house, there was a long darkening creeping over from the horizon. Mrs. Muller met them at the door with a funny little smile. She acted flustered and Otto put the milk bucket down and blinked at her with a quizzical expression. She beckoned them into the kitchen and Shan saw the whiskey jug on the table among the plates. He crossed the room and helped himself. It burned like hot coal all the way down but brightened his mood. Otto came over, poured himself a drink, and downed it.

"What're you up to?" he asked his wife.

When she made no answer, both men turned to look at her. At that moment Mary entered the kitchen from the front of the house. Otto looked over and said: "Well!" Shan turned his head, too.

Mary wasn't wearing her beaded dress. She had on a gingham one that seemed to hang low and close. It wasn't particularly attractive, that dress, but it clung and in Shan's mind his squaw was suddenly, astoundingly beautiful. There was no other word for it. She was a person, a human being. The neckline was primly high and square but the thrusting below it was unmistakable. Farther down the dress flattened out, fell inward a little over flat muscles. Mrs. Muller had gathered Mary's abundance of ebony hair up tightly behind her head, tied a ribbon around it, and left the residue to ripple down her back. Shan's ears roared with a surge of blood. He got red and confused and turned away from her, and so did not notice the way her black eyes followed him.

"See," Mrs. Muller said triumphantly, "she's pretty. You hadn't ought to call her a squaw."

Shan poured another glass of whiskey and his hand shook.

"Now let's eat," Otto said. He was frowning just the smallest bit and watching Shan.

At supper Mary was silent as usual. She had learned from observation, and Mrs. Muller, how to handle a knife and fork. Shan looked at her once when her head was bowed and noticed something he'd never seen before. The girl had brushed her hair, which she did as often as she could, until it shone, parted it evenly down the middle, and right down the part she'd daubed something red, like rouge. He was fascinated and finally said something about it to Otto.

"They do that," Otto said. "Most of them. It's sort of dress-up to them."

The meal continued, and afterward they talked a little, while the women did the dishes, cleaned up. Otto urged Shan to have a final drink before they retired. It warmed him, made him drop off to sleep as soon as he hit the bed later on. It also made him dream.

First it was Sarahlee. She was bareheaded, bare-armed, even barefooted. She was holding him close and laughing up into his face. Teasing him about something he couldn't understand. He threw his arms around her, felt the muscles in his arms bulge, and saw the hurt in her eyes. Her heavy lips got twisted and ugly and she fought him, went away from him, and stayed away. When she finally came back, she slapped him—hard—then she turned and ran. He chased her, caught her close to the new barn, threw her down in the grass, and held her. She slapped him again, so hard he closed his eyes. When he opened them again, it wasn't Sarahlee—it was Mary—and she didn't slap him. Didn't struggle at all. He watched the sunlight burn in her ebony hair, saw how round, how unblinking and still her eyes were. The way her mouth was open a little, the teeth showing white, small, and strong. Then he awakened and it was daylight out.

Otto banged the milk bucket against the side of the house, and Shan got up, climbed into his clothes, and hurried outside. The air was like perfume, full of coolness, the scent of flowers, curing grass and cleanliness. He washed at the pump, set the big black hat on the back of his head, and hastened out to help with the chores. Otto was milking. He was whistling, something Shan had never heard him do before. When he saw Shan, he grinned.

"You're going to sweat a mite today," he said. "Before tonight you'll think I'm trying to get all my time back out of you in one day. You'll see whether I'm offering you charity or not."

Shan climbed to the loft, began forking down feed. "Suits me," he said, and for a while he worked in silence. As he was coming back down the ladder, he said: "Otto, I got to say this, but

103

I'm no good at it, either. I want you to know how much I appreciate . . ."

Otto interrupted. "Wait," he said. "Just wait until we're through with those damned cattle. You'll wish you were back soldiering again."

Shan smiled. "I wouldn't wish that no matter what," he said. "I wouldn't even wish that on the redskin that burned my barn . . . not on anyone."

Otto nodded, his smile dwindling. "I expect it was bad," he said.

"Bad? You've got no idea, Otto. Men walking around tripping over their own entrails. Hanging themselves. Blowing out their brains. Dying in the rain . . . drowning, Otto . . . damned rain water running up their noses and drowning them because they were too weak to roll over." He walked swiftly to the doorway, stood in it, staring at the clean sunlight. Behind him Otto finished milking, arose, hung up the stool, and nudged Shan out into the yard.

"Come on. We've got a big day ahead of us. You got to learn to use a rope, too."

Mary was bending over the table when they entered the kitchen. Mrs. Muller looked up and smiled at them both. Her hair was drawn back into a very tight bun; it looked very plain and severe to Shan. He nodded to Mary and sat down at the table. They ate, then Mrs. Muller got up and began doing the dishes. Mary helped her. She avoided Shan. He and Otto went back outside. Mrs. Muller called to them through the door.

"We'll come out there in a minute, Otto."

Shan looked puzzled. "Does she help?"

"Sure. Until you came along she was the best helper I ever had. At marking time she's better'n most men, anyway. Let's get the corrals closed and the fires going."

Out behind the barn where the corrals were, Otto closed the gates and showed Shan where he wanted the branding fires built. It was still cool back there. Otto roped the first calf while Shan got the irons hot. Otto showed him how to tilt the irons downward so heat wouldn't travel up the handles.

"Go down the rope," he told Shan, "and throw him."

Shan tried but the calf was wild and like greased lightning. Twice he fell in the manure and both times the calf landed on top and wriggled free. Otto showed him how to do it—go down the rope, reach over the calf, get flesh holds under the flank and just aft of the off side front leg, bend his knees, and lift at the same time. The calf was lying at his feet, slammed down hard. It grunted but lay still. Otto whipped out a pigging string, wrapped the four legs, and stood up. He was breathing heavily.

"Like that," he said. "Now for the iron."

By the time the women came out, they had branded four calves and altered two that had been bulls. Shan was dirtier than he had been in several years but he'd gotten the hang of throwing them. Otto showed him how to brand, to keep the iron hot but not cherry-red or the mark would heal into a blur. Mrs. Muller took over the fire, showed Mary about tilting the irons, keeping them in the heart of the fire and not getting them too hot, how to test them on a slab of wood before handing them to the men. If they flamed when they touched the wood, they were too hot, had to be allowed to cool.

Mary learned fast. Her thick black hair had a narrow band around it; she looked more Indian than ever, and when she moved, it was with a lithe, supple grace. When she bent to hand Shan an iron, he could look past the prim neckline of her dress, see that the flesh was golden-colored.

Otto showed him how to tie calves, especially the bull calves because they struggled and bawled when they were altered. When they bled, Otto showed Shan his mistakes, explained that when they were cut right there was very little bleeding. Shan tightened his face in concentration, his expression leaving no doubt that he did not like what he was doing.

"There ought to be another way," he said. "That must hurt like the devil, Otto."

"Naw, you see they don't know, so it don't last long with them. A day or two and they're as frisky as ever . . . steers."

"Gold watern . . . Shan?"

He twisted and looked down at her. Her face was flushed from the branding fire and she was smiling up at him with the faintest lilt to her lips. He knew he looked a sight, trousers stiff with filth, hair tousled, shirt dark and limp with sweat. He grinned back. "No thanks."

Otto took the dipper, drained it, and handed it back without looking at her. "Here," he said to Shan, "you catch the next one. Hold it like this."

By the purest fluke Shan roped the first calf he made a cast at. Since he did not know how to brace against three hundred pounds of frenzied animal, when the calf hit the end of the rope, he was jerked down. Mrs. Muller smiled at her husband. Mary watched Shan struggle to his feet with the rope still in his hands and fight his way down it to the animal, reach over, and bust it. It took a long time for Shan to get the legs tied securely. Otto stood by with the faintly smoking iron. When Shan finally arose, shook sweat off his chin, Otto applied the iron. The calf emitted a wild bellow and from beyond the closest corral bars an old cow answered anxiously.

They worked until the sun was directly overhead, then sat down in the shade to rest while Mary and Otto's wife opened bundles they'd brought from the house.

"You got your pipe?" Otto asked, holding his own pipe.

"No, just some papers," Shan said, fashioning a cigarette, letting the smoke trickle upward from his nose.

"First time I ever did this," Otto said musingly, "I got kicked square in the belly. I thought all my insides were busted. It takes a lot of practice. Lots of it." He pointed the pipe at a skittering young heifer, rolling, fat and dark red. "That's one of your heifers. When she calves, you'll want to have your rope handy because an unmarked calf wandering round will wind up wearing someone else's brand on it before it's very big. We don't want any Blessing calves sucking Muller cows."

"I'll watch them."

"I know you will," Otto said, and sat there, just looking at his cattle for a while. Finally he began to rummage in a shirt pocket, drew out a shred of blue cloth with a cracked bone button sewn to it. "Here," he said to Shan, "keep this. Someday I'll tell you the story about it."

Shan held up the fragment, looking at it. It apparently had come from a man's shirt. The cloth was heavy but well-worn and faded. "What about it?"

"Just keep it," Otto said, and craned his neck when he saw the women approaching them. "Ahhhh! I could eat the tail off a skunk."

Shan put the little scrap of cloth into his pocket and forgot about it when the women spread out a cloth and put food upon it. Mary had the jug of whiskey. She set it squarely in front of Shan. Otto noticed and looked up quickly at her. Mrs. Muller smiled.

"She must think you need strong medicine," she said with a twinkle.

Shan poured some liquor into a cup and drank it. It felt good all the way down. Otto reached for the jug.

"You probably look like a buck just off the war trail to her, all bloody and dirty like you are."

"I feel like one," Shan said.

Mrs. Muller had two cushions. She handed one to Mary who held it with perplexity until she saw Mrs. Muller place hers upon the ground and sit upon it, then she did likewise. Shan repressed a grin.

Otto said: "They've got saddle-galls on their rears an inch thick from riding bareback all their lives. I bet she never sat on a cushion before." Mrs. Muller shot a dagger look at her husband. He shrugged. "She don't know that much English, Georgia."

"You'd be surprised how much she knows . . . you and Shan. I never saw anyone learn so quickly." Mrs. Muller's look softened. "If you'd take a little time with her, Shan, you'd have her talking good by the time Sarahlee gets back."

Shan took two biscuits, popped one into his mouth, and held the other one in his hand. "I'll let Sarahlee do that," he said. "I wouldn't know how to begin." He looked at the cattle. "Now I know what you mean," he said to Otto, "about this taking a week and the time passing. I'll sleep like a log tonight."

Otto spat out a piece of gristle, nodded, and glanced sideways at Shan's trousers. "If Sarahlee could see you now . . . ," he began, and didn't finish it.

"How did she get that name?" Mrs. Muller asked. "It's two names in one."

"I don't know. In the South lots of folks name their kids with two names like that, some of them even name the girls after their fathers."

"But she isn't a Southerner, is she?"

Shan frowned at the cattle. "I don't know but I don't think so." He was thinking that actually he knew very little about his wife. But he brightened when he remembered that she knew very little about him, too. That made it all right.

CHAPTER TEN

The last day they worked the cattle, Otto said he thought Shan ought to ride up and see how his horses were, if everything was all right. Shan borrowed Otto's big bay saddle horse because the buggy mare wasn't broken to ride. He left Mary at the Mullers'.

It was a beautiful afternoon with fragrance in the

air strong enough to lean against. He rode part way in an easy lope. Otto's horse was like riding a rocking chair; he wasn't young, but he was wise, which was more valuable in a cow horse. Shan wore his pistol for the first time in almost a week. Its weight was unaccustomed, dragging at his waist. From time to time he hitched irritably at his pants.

The horses were grazing about a mile north of the spring in back of the barn. He drove them south, past the cabin, and left them to drift. It was all right for them to be that far north, but he thought it likely the Blessings would be turning out soon and didn't want his horses running with their stock, especially since he hadn't branded any of them yet and Otto had let enough drop about the neighbors he'd never met to make him cautious.

When he entered the cabin, it smelled stuffy. An enterprising wood rat had begun a nest behind the stove. Among the articles he found in the débris was an old, sweat-curled pair of gloves, the pencil he'd used to write Sarahlee, a worn-out sock, and a wash rag. He cleaned the cabin, swept the earth floor, and scattered the refuse beyond the door with his boot toe. Over where he'd buried the Indian the ground had sunk a little. He looked at the spot, thinking he'd have to fill it up a little before Sarahlee saw it; she'd probably dislike the idea of an Indian buried that close to the cabin.

He went to the barn. There were several new

bird nests overhead whose occupants fled at the sound of his spurs. The sides showed dull-yellow sap oozing from cracks and slashes in the logs. He rubbed his palm up and down a big peeled log he and Otto had set as the east corner post.

It was lazily still and peaceful at the ranch. What sounds there were came from the trees and from the grass at his feet—browning a little, curling downward a mite. It was so pleasant he lay full length in the grass and let the sun bake loose the knots in his muscles. He was drowsing, thinking of nothing at all when he heard a horse whinny. He raised his head above the grass and looked around. Out where he'd left his horses he could see them standing motionlessly, heads up and alert. He rolled over, propped his head up, and studied the countryside. Two riders were coming, slouching along, riding easy and slow. They looked a lot alike, what he could make out of them. Both were tall, thin men, ungainly-looking, unkempt, and hawkish. He watched them go toward his cabin, stop in front of it. One of them said something pointing at the open door. The other one drew up in his saddle, looking around. Shan got up out of the grass and walked toward them. One he recognized from two hundred feet away. It was the bearded man he'd knocked down his first day in Tico. The same man he'd faced that night at Sarahlee's uncle's cabin. He stopped when he was close enough and nodded.

"Howdy."

The man he recognized gazed at Shan strangely for a moment, then gave an almost imperceptible nod in return. The other man, possibly a year or two younger, did not nod at all. "You the feller lives here?" he asked scratchily.

"Yes," Shan said, taking an instant dislike to the second man. "Who're you?"

"Neighbors. I'm Art Blessing. This is my brother Amos."

"I've met Amos before," Shan said. "What do you want?" Everything he'd ever heard came back very clearly. Remembering Amos from two unpleasant meetings didn't help the way he felt now, either.

"Well, hell," Art Blessing said, "you ain't a real friendly cuss, are you?"

Amos shifted his weight in the saddle. Both his hands lay indolently upon the saddle horn. He spat aside and worked his jaws rhythmically.

"I said what do you want?"

"Nice new barn you got there. Too bad about the other one." Art Blessing's head was tilted back a little. He was looking down his nose at Shan on the ground. "What burned it . . . you know?"

"Indians burned it," Shan said, and tipped his head toward the sunken place in the yard. "One of them's buried there."

Both Blessings regarded Shan steadily for a moment, then exchanged a glance. Amos smiled,

113

spat again. "Real hell roarer, ain't you, soldier?"

"You ought to know."

Amos retained his smile. "Yeah, I ought to," he said. "Only I don't. I was drunk that night in the saloon last winter." His beard shone rusty in the sunlight. "And say, soldier, if you ever want to know about Sarahlee Gordon, just ask me. Don't bother callin' on her . . . just ask me."

Shan's face darkened. "You wouldn't know anything," he said flatly. "You don't even know enough to wash your whiskers."

Amos's smile dissolved. One hand moved off the saddle horn. Art Blessing made a short, choppy laugh. "Better not roil him, Amos," he said. "He's big and tough. All them Abe Lincoln boys're big and tough."

"Next time you ride down this way," Shan said, "keep out on the road."

"Or?" Amos asked.

"Or you'll wish you had."

The Blessings sat still, looking down at him. They were no longer smiling. There was a stillness to their faces, a cold, calculating stillness.

"Rider coming," Art Blessing said softly to his brother.

All three men looked up. A solitary horseman was swinging toward them across the range a long way east of the road. They watched for a while, then Art Blessing raised his rein hand.

"Let's go," he said to his brother. "Listen, squatter," he said to Shan, "we don't use that road. Never have, never goin' to. If you don't like it, why just put on your war paint and look us up. We live north there a few miles."

They rode off, angling westerly and watching the oncoming rider. Shan looked after them. He knew, then, that only the advent of the rider had kept them from shooting him. It was a sobering realization.

He thought of Amos's words about Sarahlee. They ate into his mind like acid, left him filled with dark, torturing questions. Now Amos's smile seemed secretive, mocking. He clenched his fists hard; the next time they met he promised himself one of them was going to get hurt.

The Blessings rode leisurely out and around the rider, and stopped. Shan watched them turn their horses, stare as the rider swung past, and very faintly he heard one of them call out— "Squawman. . . ."—throw up an arm in a sneering way, and ride on.

He wasn't certain what they meant until he recognized one of Otto's horses. A second later he saw the wind-whipped sheen of raven-black hair. Mary. He turned his head to follow the brothers and his face was savage-looking. When the girl drew up and stopped, he turned angrily on her, but something unusual held him from speaking. Mary was riding side-saddle. That reminded him of what Otto had said about Indians riding bareback all their lives—about having saddle-galls an inch thick, and he lowered his eyes in embarrassment. She *had* understood.

She dismounted, stood beside the horse a moment, then reached up and brought a little bundle down from the saddle and held it out toward him.

He took it, puzzled, opened it, and saw the food. "Well," he said, the turbulence dying. "Missus Muller send this?"

"I bring it. You hungry."

He folded the cloth and handed it back to her. "You eat it. I'm not hungry. What did they send you for?"

"I come myself," she said, taking the bundle but making no move to open it.

"Oh? Why?"

She did not reply. Something hot and unpleasant erupted in Shan's throat. He turned away, squinted out where the Blessings could no longer be seen, then started walking out where he'd left his horses.

The animals moved away from him, watching in a sidling way, wary but not actually fearful. The grass was thick where he swished through it. He noticed the horses were too fat. A little breeze ruffled his hair, left a dark lock hanging over his forehead. He stood there in the sun, watching an enormous bank of clouds moving majestically

116

across the sky from the north. Below, on the ground, a series of cloud shadows, gray and mottled, trailed after them.

What had Blessing meant about Sarahlee? He wished he could do it over again; he'd pull him off the horse, beat him senseless. He turned, let the sun smash him across the face with its full force. He had to squint to see the cabin and the yard. The shiny barn danced in waves of heat. Looking at it, he suddenly recalled something. In that first wagonload from Tico he'd brought a jug of rye whiskey. He had buried it near the spring box in the cool, dark mud. Until this minute he'd completely forgotten it. His throat got moist thinking about it. He started toward the barn. If those thieving Indians hadn't found it . . .

If you ever want to know about Sarahlee Gordon, just ask me.

He sat down near the spring box. The ground was damp and cool. He smoothed out the weeds and grass, pulled at them, held up a handful of tall grass, and peered at the heads. They were cured, dropping and shriveled, reminding him of what Otto had said. For the first time he understood fully what drought was. It made him forget the whiskey for the moment, feel hollow and fearful because drought was something he could not combat. Like the siege of cholera they'd had at the Reb prison he'd helped liberate. The smell had been awful; it rose up out of the ground, clung to

117

the trees and lay in the grass. A man can't fight things like that. Cholera or drought.

Due north were the purple mountains. They looked cool, well-watered. Why couldn't they drive the cattle up there, if the feed gave out down below? They'd have to cross Blessing range, of course. He dropped the grass. He'd like to cross Blessing range, maybe meet Amos there—kill him, maybe.

He stood up with a curse. He stood there with the horses far out behind him, the huge clouds drifting overhead, the lift and roll of Wyoming flowing outward and forever all around him. *Why didn't she come back, dammit!* Her paw was sick—well, so was her husband sick! Sick and tired of waiting, of yearning. He looked at the dark earth and remembered why he'd walked there, bent down, and hooked taloned fingers into the moist soil, and pulled it away. A horse blew its nose off to his left somewhere and he whirled. It was the animal Mary had ridden over; she'd tied it among the scrub oaks. He stared at it with the cool jug in his hands, then looked down, began to worry the plug out of the crock.

When he went to the cabin later, Mary looked different to him. He couldn't define it and didn't dwell upon it, but it remained a fact he was conscious of. The cabin smelled good, his coffee pot was boiling on the stove, and Mary looked around at him but her face was blank. Without a

118

word she filled one of the graniteware cups and placed it on the table, then she opened the oven and brought out a laden dish, set it beside the cup.

He sat down and ate. Mary stayed over by the stove. She was cleaning up. When he finished, he went back outdoors, smoked his pipe, and except for that one thin little persistent thought the world seemed like a good place.

Mary came outside and started across the yard. Shan watched her. There wasn't an ounce of bouncy fat on her anywhere. She walked very erect, very proud; it made him smile. A proud Indian. A proud bitch Indian. Pint-sized squaw. The thoughts hurt, though; he let them die. She wasn't a squaw, she was a girl—a lovely girl. No, she was a kid. That made him feel better, more mellow as though he looked down from a pinnacle of wisdom and years, recognized her as a youngster. He even forgot Amos Blessing.

"Hey, Mary, where are you going?"

She stopped and turned. Sideways her stomach was as flat as an iron skillet. Up higher—no, the illusion was spoiled; she wasn't a child. "Get watern," she said.

He smiled and arose, walked lazily down where she was, took the bucket from her hand, and started toward the spring. "I'll help you," he said. "Come along."

The spring box was made of logs. It had been one of the first things he and Otto had built

119

together. It was mossy around it, cool and muddy. He stooped, filled the bucket, and held it out to her. She set it down and stood in front of him, looking up into his face. He was aware of some wild scent. It took a moment for him to realize it came from her. It smelled like crushed mint leaves with maybe pine needles blended into it. No, not mint, sweet grass and pine needles, that's what it was.

"Mary, you've got perfume on."

She shook her head, signifying that she did not understand.

"Scent . . . perfume." He took the bucket up roughly and started briskly across the yard. She walked beside him. He put the bucket down just inside the doorway, took her arm, and started across the yard where two shaggy pine trees stood, out a ways. There he scooped up some needles, crushed them in his fist, and smelled them.

"Sure, I thought that's what it was . . . pine scent and sweet grass. It smells good." He held out his fingers. She touched her nose to his palm, wrinkled it, and smiled at him, then she lowered her head so he could see the red mark down the part of her hair. "Oh, that's how you wear it," he said. "Even squaws like to smell good."

Her face grew instantly blank, all animation left it, and she moved away from him, crossed the yard to the washstand outside the cabin, and stood there in the shade, looking out where the horses were.

He walked over near her. "Hey, Mary . . . I forgot you learned so much English. I'm sorry, honest."

"Injun squaw," she said without turning to face him. "Damned stinking Injun squaw!"

He was shocked speechless; a moment later he burst into laughter. "Say," he said gleefully, "you're learning more'n Missus Muller's teaching you, Mary. You've got to quit hanging around where Otto and I're working." He thought of the consequences if she said something like that around the Mullers or Sarahlee and the mirth went out of him. He turned her by the shoulders and used his fingers to emphasize what he told her. "Listen, Mary, don't ever say 'damned' or 'stinking' around other people, especially around a white woman . . . understand?"

The black eyes clung to his face. "Why you come up here?" She asked solemnly, and it was so far from what he was trying to explain that he drew up and stared.

"Oh, you mean today . . . you mean why did I come up here today?"

"Yes."

"Well, to look after the horses . . . sort of see how things were . . . do a little thinking."

"To pray?" The black eyes were soft now, soft and understanding.

121

"Pray? Hell no, kid, I don't pray. Why should I pray? I got this." He swung his arm in a large sweep. "I got all I want. . . ." The vision of Sarahlee, of Amos Blessing standing between them, leaped up out of nowhere. He dropped the arm. "Come on, we've got to get back. Go get your horse."

They rode down through the slanting afternoon light in complete silence, and Mary seemed contented that it was to be that way. While they were still a mile or so north of the witness tree, Shan heard faint shouts and the lowing of driven cattle. He reined up. The sound swelled from the west. A billowing dust cloud and a large herd of cattle moved inexorably toward them.

Shan frowned, watching. Turn-out time. That part he understood, but if those cattle kept on the way they were headed, they'd roll over his land. He watched a solitary rider lope out ahead, on the point of the herd. Without thinking of Mary, he whirled Otto's big bay and roweled him into a long lope. Mary followed after him. When he knew the point rider had seen him, he drew up and waited.

When the cowboy halted, he was smiling through a layer of dust and sweat. "Howdy," he said genially, eyes sweeping past Shan to the Indian girl. They widened a trifle before they went back to Shan's face.

"Where are you taking those cattle?"

"Turning 'em out," the rider said.

"I can see that, but *where* are you turning them out?"

"Oh," the cowboy said carelessly, "east of the stage road somewhere. Why?"

"Because I own east of the road and I've got my own cattle to think about feeding."

"You own it?" the rider said, surprised and interested.

"Yes. There's a cabin and a new barn a mile north from here. That's my place. I own from there south to the juniper tree near Otto Muller's place."

"Oh," the cowboy said. "Well, we didn't know anyone'd taken up that land." He gazed speculatively at Shan. "I did hear something last winter . . . something about a soldier taking up land in here somewhere."

"That's me."

"Well, that makes a difference then."

"I've got to save that grass."

"Sure, mister. Well, I guess I'd better point 'em north then. We didn't know." He grinned again. "My name's Ash O'Brien. My paw's Will O'Brien. I'm right glad to know you."

Shan shook the hand and dropped it. "I'm Ryan Shanley. Folks call me Shan."

"Proud to know you, Shan. Well, I'd better head 'em away. See you in town sometime."

Shan watched him ride away, turn the lead

cattle, and when two other riders swirled up out of the dust, Shan could make out their faintly inquiring shouts. He watched the three men come together, sit there motioning and talking for a moment, then all three of them turned and looked down where he was. He reined back toward the road and saw Mary behind him. Until then he'd forgotten her completely.

He rode back as far as the road and headed southward. Something urged him to look back. The three cowboys were rocking back and forth in their saddles like they were laughing. He watched a moment and a slow burn crept into his face. He guessed what they were laughing about, a little Indian girl following a big white man around away out here. Squawman . . . !

CHAPTER ELEVEN

When they rode into the yard, Otto was sitting in the shade by the barn, oiling harness. He nodded without speaking and continued to work until Mary had put up her horse and gone toward the house, then he knocked out his pipe and leaned over the hitch rail where the dark, oil straps hung.

"Shan, did you tell Mary to go up to your place today?"

Shan finished hanging up Otto's saddle before

he replied. "No, I thought at first Missus Muller sent her with that food."

Otto rubbed his forehead with the back of his hand and looked troubled. "I figured it was something like that. No, Georgia didn't say anything to her. She just took that horse and skinned out of here."

An uncomfortable idea was forming in Shan's mind. "What would make her do a thing like that?"

"You," Otto said bluntly. "I know you think Mary'd be handy for Sarahlee around the place, but, son, I expect you ought to get rid of her."

"You think she's sweet on me?"

"That's exactly what I think. Why hasn't she run away? Why's she always staring at you? Why'd she run after you today? Now, for my part, I know it's none of my business and all. But I got a little more savvy of these things than you have, I think, and even if I'm wrong, it won't hurt any. I expect Sarahlee'd rather do her own sewing and what-not anyway, so before something comes of this, why don't you just get rid of her?"

Shan leaned on the rail beside Otto, dwarfing him. "Does Missus Muller think that, too?" he asked.

"She doesn't know Mary slipped off today. I just said I let her have a horse to go for a ride. I wasn't sure until I saw you two coming down the road together, you see. I had suspicions . . . have had 'em for some time now . . . but, anyway, what's the sense of worrying Georgia? She thinks a lot of that little squaw."

Shan winced. "Well, I didn't have anything to do with her coming up there today," he said.

"If I thought that," Otto said, "I'd also think you were the biggest damned fool in the world. Sarahlee's really something fit for a man to look at, but that little squaw . . ."

"But getting rid of her . . ."

Otto jerked off the rail abruptly. "I almost forgot," he said. "I got a letter for you." He fished inside his shirt and drew out the envelope. "It's from Sarahlee." Shan took it. "One of the O'Brien boys was going by and left it."

"I met an O'Brien up by my place," Shan said, looking at the envelope. "They had a big drive, and when I told them I needed my grass this year, they turned north." He tore the envelope and pulled out the letter. His hands were shaking.

"She's coming, Otto."

"When?"

"Let's see. Four days from now. Four more days."

Otto wiped his hands on his trousers. "Come on, Georgia'll want to know this. Besides, it's about time for a little celebration."

They celebrated well and good, all through supper and afterward, until Otto's wife went off to bed and Mary disappeared upstairs somewhere. When Otto staggered off after his wife, he gave

Shan's shoulder a resoundingly affectionate slap as he rolled past.

Shan sat in the soft light until after midnight, alternated between feeling good, and sorry for himself, and sweating in anticipation. Then he retired.

The next three days were torture. Twice Shan rode to the cabin to clean things up. The third time he heard someone coming and went outside. It was the Blessing brothers. Shan had left his pistol hanging inside. The Blessings stopped in the yard as they'd done before and measured him with their eyes.

"Howdy, soldier boy. Looks like you're fixin' the place up for a weddin'."

"Maybe you fellers didn't understand me when I said not to ride across here any more . . . to use the road."

"Sure," Amos said, "we understood you, only we're in the habit of crossin' through here. You got anything to say to that?"

Shan wasn't angry, just annoyed. "Well," he said, "if that's the way you want it, why I expect you might as well climb down off that horse."

Art Blessing drew his pistol in a slow, lazy way and lay it barrel first across the saddle horn. "The last time you made that kind of talk," he said, "your squaw came ridin' up and saved you from gettin' hurt. She ain't around now . . . or is she? You got her inside?"

Shan made no answer and his face was brick-red. Wrath was boiling in him.

"Sure he has," Amos said. "Let's let it ride, Art. We'll catch him alone one of these times. Let's go."

Art holstered his gun in the same contemptuous way. "All right. Maybe worryin' about the next time'll soften him up a little. What d'you think, soldier boy . . . squawman?"

Shan said nothing. They exchanged cold glances for a moment, then the Blessings rode off. Shan watched them with contempt for himself, anger over his carelessness in being caught unarmed, making him bitter. When he rode back to the Mullers' place that night, ate supper, and went outside for a pipe, Otto trailed after him. They sat in the cool dusk with the scent from the barn coming down to them.

"What's bothering you, boy? You didn't say two words all through supper."

Shan told him about the Blessings. Went further back and told of his earlier meeting with them, what Amos had hinted about Sarahlee.

Otto sucked on his pipe for a moment, eyes like small, wet pebbles. "I see," he said. "Well, I expect it's time to tell you something, Shan."

"Huh?"

"I got a confession to make to you."

"Otto, there wasn't another letter, was there? She's still coming tomorrow, isn't she?"

"Yes, as far as I know she's coming tomorrow, all right. It isn't that, son. You recollect that little piece of cloth I gave you with the bone button on it?"

"I've got it in my pocket. What about it?"

"Well, when we were re-building the barn, I was poking around and found that thing snagged on a nail out by the corral."

Shan was holding the button and its scrap of cloth in his hand. "What about it, Otto?"

"You can't figure it out, can you? Shan, it wasn't Indians set fire to that barn. Indians don't wear blue work shirts with bone buttons."

Shan's fist closed slowly around the relic. He looked squarely into Otto's face.

"You've met your neighbors, Shan. Which ones wear blue shirts with bone buttons, O'Briens or Blessings?"

"Why didn't you tell me before?"

"I'm older'n you, Shan. I know the different kinds of men there are. When you saw that ruined barn and those Indians poking around, you went sort of crazy. You didn't even stop to think three Indians with carbines were greater odds than an ordinary man'd go up against with just one pistol. After you'd killed the Indians . . . if you'd found out it was the Blessings set that fire, you'd have gone after them the same way. They'd have killed you deader than you killed those Indians. They would have been expecting you, for they knew damned well who set that fire and how you'd feel if you had any idea it was them. That's why I kept it from you until you'd had time to calm down a little."

"You don't think I'll go after them now, Otto?"

Otto knocked out his pipe against the horny palm of his hand. "It's too late, Shan. You've got a new and better barn to start with. You've got a wife now, too. You wouldn't want to make her a widow . . . never see her again. And, Shan, what's past is past."

"If you feel that way, why did you tell this at all?"

"Because, like I've always thought, someday you and the Blessings were going to lock horns. I've tried to make you understand that they are dangerous men . . . killers. You never paid much attention to that. Now you will . . . now you'll know how low they'll stoop and what they'll do to you if they ever get the chance. After this you'll watch out, and if it ever comes to shooting, you'll get behind the biggest rock and shoot first."

Shan retired with the knowledge of the Blessings' treachery eating away at his mind. The longer he lay there, the further he was from sleep and the more he re-lived all that backbreaking labor he and Otto had been forced to do over again. The killing of the Southern Cheyennes pricked his conscience. No wonder they hadn't fired back. They hadn't wanted to fight, hadn't

130

any idea why the big, crazy white man lit into them like a madman.

Hours later, when the house was still and dark, he got up, sat on the edge of the bed, and smoked a cigarette, then he deliberately got dressed, carried his boots into the kitchen before putting them on, drank some dregs of coffee, took Otto's carbine from a moonlit corner, and went outside.

At the barn the horses snorted at him. It was dark inside where the saddles hung. He saddled and bridled the wise old bay, swung up, and rode off. The sway of his pistol felt good on his hip, for once its dragging weight wasn't annoying.

He rode due north but paralleling the road, not out upon it. The lariat on Otto's saddle made a handy place to carry the carbine. He had no clear idea what he was going to do. He hoped the Blessings would be at his place, maybe skulking around, getting ready to fire the barn again. But they weren't.

Moonlight flooded the yard by the cabin. He sat out a ways, watching the haunted stillness for a long time, then he struck out north again. Beyond the farthest land swell was Blessing range. He'd never seen the home ranch buildings but knew approximately where they were. He rode steadily until he topped out over the last thin fingering of a ridge and saw the dark, square shapes that were buildings. Face to face with the need to make a decision, he couldn't. The house was warped and set amid a profusion of shaggy little trees and scrub flowers. Beyond was the low, large barn. It was a disappointment to see that it was mud and log construction. Even if he fired it, it wouldn't burn enough to hurt.

While he sat there, wondering and watching, a coyote yelped. The cry ended in a high, drawn-out and choked-off sort of howl. Several dogs answered from the yard down below and Shan knew he could never get close enough to fire the barn or the house, either, without the dogs discovering him, raising an alarm.

He turned and rode back toward his own place. Halfway down the far slope he saw a little band of drowsing cattle. A few were standing up, but mostly they were lying upon the ground, sleeping or chewing cuds. There were several blurs close by the cows that would be calves. A young Durham bull, much better bred than the cows, leaped up at sight of the horse and rider and made a thumping sound. He didn't have much horn, but he dropped his head threateningly and shook what he did have. The cows were shaggy, rangy, slab-sided, and bucket-hipped. Shan rode as close as he dared and stopped. He thought they might be O'Brien cattle until the little bull swung broadside and he saw the new pink scar along the ribs in a large letter B. Then an idea came to him. The Blessings had undoubtedly paid a lot of money for that high-bred young bull. He would be something they prized very highly. He knew that roping that wild young bull and roping calves in Otto's corral were altogether different things. Well, this was about what he wanted. It wouldn't cripple the Blessings like burning his barn had crippled him, but for the time being it would suffice. He eased down the rope and started the big bay horse forward, chased the little bull a full three quarters of a mile before he made a good cast. By then he was a long way southward and Otto's big bay horse was winded. The other cattle had scattered like birds.

Otto's big horse could hold the bull but Shan had no idea how he was going to throw him, let alone tie his legs. There was a stripling fir tree close by, which he rode around twice, then dismounted, and made the rope fast to. He left the bay horse to watch and started down the rope, then he stopped. Even if he could get hold of the bull without being trampled in a charge, he couldn't throw him without a second lariat, which he did not have.

Then the little bull choked himself down fighting the rope, fell over on his side, eyes rolling back and tongue lolling. The sound of his shallow breathing was painful to hear. Shan picked up a large rock and walked forward. The bull didn't move; his eyes were rolled back under the lids and bloodshot. He began to quiver and shake, then he got rigid for a moment and went limp all over. Shan dropped the rock and bent over him, tugged at the taut rope until he got enough slack for air to pass the beast's throat, enter his windpipe. The animal was unconscious. Shan grabbed his knife and went to work. He tied off the cords with two twisted hairs yanked from the bull's tail, removed the lariat, coiled it as he went toward Otto's horse, mounted, secured the rope, and made a cigarette. His hands were as steady as lead. The exertion more than the deed made him feel better. He saw the bull raise his head and let it fall back several times, until finally he held it up, then Shan turned and rode back the way he had come. When he arrived back at the barn, he put the bay horse up, went inside to his room, and lay on the bed fully clothed. He fell asleep almost instantly.

CHAPTER TWELVE

The next morning Otto had all the chores done by the time Shan got out to the barn. When Shan stepped through the door, he saw Otto leaning on a pitchfork, staring at his bay horse. He turned and looked slit-eyed at Shan.

"Did you go for a ride last night?" he asked suspiciously.

"Yes," Shan said candidly.

"What did you do?" Otto's grip on the pitchfork was painfully tight.

"Rode up by Blessing place."

"The barn, Shan?"

"No, they've got a pack of hounds up there. I found a pure bred bull . . ."

"You cut him?"

"Yes."

Otto's hands relaxed a little. "Did you tie off the cords? I've seen that little bull. He'll die if you didn't tie them off. He's too old for Barlow-knife cutting."

"I did it like you showed me on the big calves."

Otto turned away, hung the pitchfork up, took down the full milk bucket, and started for the house. Shan hastened to catch up. "You understand, don't you, Otto?"

"Yes, I understand, but it's going to be the start of things, too. They'll find him today, probably ride down here when they don't find you up there." Otto stopped stockstill. "We das'n't go down to Tico today for Sarahlee."

"What? Why not?"

"I expect Georgia and Mary can go. Why not? Because, like I just said, they'll come looking for you. If no one's around, they'll burn us *both* out. You can't do something like that, then go away, Shan." Otto started forward again. "You didn't think, Shan. You should have waited a few days. No, maybe not, maybe it's better to have it now than after Sarahlee's up there with you."

"Sarahlee won't like it, me not meeting her."

"I expect she won't," Otto said dryly, "but she'd

like it a lot less coming home to no cabin *and* no barn." They were close to the back of the house. "Don't say anything to Georgia about last night. I'll say we have to take a jag of hay up to your place so we can drive the heifers up tomorrow. That way she won't think it's strange you not going down to Tico."

Mrs. Muller seemed disappointed when Otto explained what he and Shan had talked of, but she didn't stay depressed long, the prospect of seeing the bride, of delivering her to Shan in person, brightened her spirits again.

After breakfast Otto and Shan hitched the team to the wagon and watched Mrs. Muller and Mary drive out of the yard. The Indian girl's face was a sharp contrast to Otto's wife's expression.

Shan and Otto immediately saddled up and struck out for the cabin. Otto had his rifle and a pistol. Shan had only the belt gun; his carbine was at the cabin. Otto did not speak until Shan said: "They might not find that bull for a week."

Otto looked grim. Up on his big bay horse, wide, massive shoulders squared into the north, face frozen in a mask of wary unpleasantness, his appearance made a better answer than his words. "I heard from Will O'Brien the Blessings bought two fine imported Durham bulls. They'll be watching over them like hawks. They'll find him all right, if not today, then tomorrow, but no later than that."

"Maybe they'll think the O'Briens cut him."

"The O'Briens have no reason, Shan, you have. Even if they thought you believed what you said about those Indians firing the barn, they'll remember you talked hard to them. No, I don't think they'll waste much time figuring who to pay back."

They swung east off the road with the sun working up a head of heat, crossed Shan's yard, and put their horses in the barn. Otto stood outside afterward studying the distant slope of land.

"They'll be along today," he said, "or I'll give you a fat steer."

They went to the cabin and for lack of something to do made a pot of coffee. Shan lit his pipe and sat on the edge of the bed. He couldn't relax or stay down long. It was like waiting for a bugler to blow you out of some woods, or call you up in the darkness to repel a cavalry attack. He smoked until his tongue was tender, then put the pipe out, went to the door, and stood in the opening, looking up toward the slope. Otto watched him for a while, then said: "Go water the horses, if you got to be moving around. Maybe they're out there watching . . . it'll give them a chance."

Shan studied the close-in country and nodded. "I wish they'd show themselves if they're out there."

"Walk outside, then," Otto said a little sharper. "Here, take your carbine along."

"I got my pistol."

Otto's voice crackled. "You take this carbine. What the hell good is a pistol at carbine range?"

Shan tucked the gun under his arm and walked across the yard and into the barn. There wasn't a sound anywhere around all the time he was crossing the open places. Otto got off the chair in the cabin and went to a little window to peer out. He stood there for a long time with his cold pipe jutting from between his teeth.

Shan was dunging out after he'd watered the horses when he heard a dog bark. For just a second his blood froze. He hung the fork up, took his carbine, and went to the little corral outside the barn facing north.

Coming down the slope were two riders. They both had carbines across the saddle forks and were bending over, looking at the ground. Four or five dogs ran ahead of them, quartering in the tall grass. Shan wondered whether the dogs were following blood marks from the little Durham bull or the spoor of Otto's bay horse. He moved away from the sunlight, stood motionlessly against the barn until they were close enough to recognize, then he sidled toward the barn door and waited there, watching.

The Blessings turned away from the yard and rode down around the barn. Shan faded into the cool, dark interior, cocked the carbine, and waited but they went on by. He crept out and watched them ride south without going near the cabin.

Clearly they were following the little bull's sign, too intent upon it to bother right then with anything else.

After they'd passed, he crossed to the cabin and met Otto in the doorway. There was glistening sweat on the older man's face and the little pipe still jutted from his mouth, forgotten.

"How far have they got to go before they find what they're looking for?" he asked Shan.

"A mile maybe. There's a skinny fir tree where I did it."

"I know that tree," Otto said. "Stands all by itself and has no limbs for about twenty feet up."

"That's right."

Otto put his rifle down and walked toward the stove. Shan watched him pour a cup of coffee and drink it, put his pipe in a pocket without knocking out the dottle. "You got any whiskey up here?" he asked.

Shan went to the bed, tossed his carbine upon it, and got down on the floor, squirmed half under the bed, and dragged out the crock of rye liquor. He had a crooked, mirthless smile on his face when he stood up and beat at the dust on the front of him.

"I forget to drink when I'm up here. Guess I'm in the habit of drinking only at your place."

Otto drank, ran a sleeve over his mouth, and went to the little window again. The sun was almost directly overhead. Otto grew rigid for a moment, then he spoke without looking back. "Here they come."

"I'll go back to the barn."

Otto nodded briskly. He was measuring the distance with his eyes. "If they see you go down there, they'll think you're alone. Go on, and remember, Shan . . . they're out to kill you any way they can. Don't get heroic about that stand-up-and-fight bunk. It's you and me . . . Art and Amos . . . first dog down and last dog hung, no quarter, no truce. Go on."

Shan had the carbine at his side when he went out. He didn't look around until he was at the spring box, then he only shot one fast glance southward and hurried on. The dogs were racing to keep up and both Blessings were riding hard straight for the barn. He didn't have to see more than the way they rode to know how furious they were. At the opening into the barn he halted again. The roll of running horses came muffled and distant but getting louder each second. He moved out of sight and waited.

He wondered why he was willing to die over a little Durham bull, decided it wasn't the bull, it was the bull's owners he was willing to die fighting. He heard them split up. One rode around the barn to get between Shan and the cabin. He thought that normally that would have been wise strategy, but with Otto watching like an Indian from within the cabin it was anything but wise now. When the sounds of horses stopped, the yard was still as death. When he cocked the carbine, it sounded like a miniature hammer striking an anvil. There wasn't even a little breeze outside, just stillness.

"Hey, soldier, come out of the barn!"

The voice was familiar, high and scratchy. It belonged to Art Blessing which meant Amos was the rider around in back of the barn, between Shan and the cabin.

"Why don't you come in here and get me?"

"We found that bull, soldier. That was the biggest mistake you ever made in your whole damned life."

"As big as you burning my barn, Blessing?"

The scratchy voice swore. "We're going to kill you for that, soldier. We're going to kill you and bury you in your own private graveyard."

"You talk too much!" Shan yelled. "I think you're too yellow to come in here and try it. Come on. I'm waiting."

It wasn't much of a gunfight. Amos was behind the barn. He crept up close and found a crack, stuck his carbine through it, and fired. The bullet sang overhead because Amos couldn't see his front sight or Shan, either. The explosion reverberated within the barn and Shan dropped flat, twisted around, seeking Amos. When the second shot came, booming in a distant way, he saw movement. Amos's rifle canted crazily upward and stayed like that. Something solid struck the back of the barn and slid down it. There was a hoarse cry of surprise from down by the spring box, then Shan heard Art yell.

"Amos? Amos, are you all right? There's someone in the cabin." When there was no reply, Art called his brother's name twice more before he grew silent.

Shan belly-crawled to the door opening, pushed his chin low in the dust, and peered out. Art Blessing was partially visible behind the logged-up spring box. Shan edged his carbine out very carefully, caught the faded britches over the sights, snuggled down, froze for a second, and fired. Art gave a leap into the air and landed in a huddle. Shan heard him making noises. It sounded like he was moaning and cursing at the same time.

Shan drew back, stood up, pressing against the inside wall of the barn with his heart slamming inside like it had broken loose. The muscle in the side of his neck jerked. There wasn't a sound outside. The louder explosion of Otto's rifle had died away, leaving a vacuum. Standing there, Shan thought with scorn of the Blessings' stupidity; Amos particularly had been stupid riding up like he had, throwing himself down with his back to the cabin. Maybe they were fast men with guns like Otto had said, but they were just plain dumb other ways and wouldn't have lasted ten days in the war—not two days.

"Hey, Blessing," he called out suddenly, "you had enough?"

Profanity, sounding pointless and choked, came back. It made Shan feel good to hear it. His eyes were large and shiny with excitement.

"I'm coming out, Blessing. If you want to fight, I'll give you a chance."

Otto's voice thundered from behind and off to one side of the cabin. "Stay in there, Shan! I can see him. I think he's hit in the arm or leg. Stay where you are. Don't get between me and him."

Shan yelled back: "Where's the other one?"

"He's dead. He's lying in plain sight at the back of the barn. You stay in there."

But Shan went around the door and out into plain sight like the Army'd taught him to do on a skirmish, not standing straight up and walking, but doubled low over his gun and moving at an angle. He kept the spring box between him and Blessing, bent extra low so the logs shielded him from sight. Moving easterly he could see Art Blessing and he was badly hurt. He didn't seem to have any fight left in him. There was a glistening splash of blood over the upper edge of the spring box on which the sun shone. Blessing was huddled up like he was ill.

When Shan was close, straightening up with the carbine pointing down at the injured man, Blessing saw him. He made no move, only his head followed Shan, his eyes sharp and compre-

143

hending. Shan's finger lay lightly around the carbine trigger as he went up and kicked Blessing's carbine away, bent, caught his pistol in one hand, and tossed it out, skittering into the hot sunlight. Then he raised his head and looked up toward the cabin. Otto was standing like a statue in the doorway with his big rifle in front of him.

"He couldn't shoot if he wanted to. Come on down, Otto."

Otto crossed the yard warily. He was dark with sweat and looked more grim and squatty than ever. He stared at the wounded man for a moment, then leaned his rifle upon the logs, and kneeled beside him without a word. Blessing's face was the color of dirty silk, his eyes squeezed so tightly closed water was forced out of them at the edges.

"Fetch some rags, Shan. He'll bleed out."

"Let him."

"Get the rags!"

Shan went toward the cabin. On his way back he detoured past the slumped body of Amos Blessing. Amos's thin frame was doubled over his carbine so far it looked like he didn't have a bone in his body. Shan bent, knocked Amos's hat off, grasped the mat of hair, and pulled back. There was no doubt after one look at the face. He let go and straightened up. Amos had never known what hit him. Otto's slug had caught him at the base of the skull and plowed upward. He went over to the spring box and handed Otto the rags. The older man began twisting them into a rope that he put around Art Blessing's shoulder. While he worked, he nodded his head at the logs.

"See that groove? It hit there first, got deflected, and went into his arm. Seems like it went downward from the shoulder and came out his elbow. The arm feels like sausage. If he don't bleed out, at least he'll never use his right hand for much."

Blessing passed out. They carried him over by the buggy and lay him in the shade. Otto brushed angrily at the blue-tailed flies that came out of nowhere and fastened themselves greedily upon Blessing's red shirt. He looked at Shan.

"Now what," he said, and it was not a question.

"Bury the one and take this other one over the hill to their house, I guess."

Otto shook his head. "No, we'll take them *both* home. Let's load Amos into the buggy first."

Amos posed no problem; they did not need to worry about his comfort. Art was placed more tenderly, so that his head lay upon his dead brother's stomach.

"What about their horses?"

"Tie them to the tailgate."

Otto put one of the Indian horses between the shafts while Shan caught the Blessings' horses, tied them, and got up onto the seat. They drove out of the yard heading toward the upland slope without a word passing between them.

When they began the long, angling descent, dogs came out of the shadows down by the Blessings' house, barking and walking stiff-legged. They drew up and called out; no one came out or answered. Otto beat on the closed door and hollow echoes came back. Shan got down and between them they carried both Blessings up onto the narrow porch. Amos they left on the ground, Art they braced against the wall, and Otto got a pail of water from over by the well and put it beside him, then they drove back.

When they halted near Shan's barn, Otto said: "We'd better sluice that blood off the spring box."

"I'll do it," Shan said, alighting.

"All right. I'll go kick some dirt over the place where Amos was."

Shan scrubbed hard. Most of the blood washed off but an uneven and dark stain remained. He patted dust over it, obscuring the outline somewhat, then went back to the buggy. Otto was removing the horse from between the shafts. When Shan walked over, he said: "Get rid of their guns, Shan."

He gathered up the weapons and looked at them. They were expensive, well-oiled weapons. He hadn't decided what to do with them by the time Otto had their horses saddled so he called to him, and, obeying, went hastily around the barn and stuck them barrels first into the manure pile.

They rode southward. Near the witness tree

Otto dug out his pipe, emptied and filled it, and lit it. "Some men just never learn," he said, tamping the pipe bowl with a thumb pad. "They've fought their share of Indians, then rode into that yard like the greenest greenhorns I ever saw."

"Our horses were hid in the barn," Shan said. "They saw me cross the yard and just figured I was alone."

"Well," Otto said, "would you go charging up like that . . . in plain sight . . . not even taking cover?"

"I guess not."

"They knew better, too. It's hard to understand."

"They just weren't thinking straight. You saw how mad they were. Say, Otto, don't they have any family? How come there was no one at the house?"

"Art's married but Amos isn't. Maybe Art's woman saw us coming and hid out. Maybe she wasn't even home. I don't know much about her, only that she's from back East somewhere."

"If she wasn't around and doesn't come back pretty soon, Art'll die."

"Maybe. You can't tell. He lost a lot of blood, but he's as tough as a boiled owl, too."

When they rode up to Otto's barn, the wagon wasn't in the yard. Otto got down and said: "I'm glad of that. It takes me a little time to act natural after something like this. Let's do the chores."

Shan fed and Otto milked, then they went

around back and closed the gates so the cattle wouldn't drift away from the barn. While they were leaning over the last gate, Otto said they'd take the heifers up to Shan's the following day. When the shadows began to draw out along the ground, they went inside and Otto brought out the whiskey jug. They sat in the gloom, drinking and talking. As the dusk settled, Otto lost his grim look, his unnatural stiffness.

"Stage must have been late," he said. "It's never on time anyway."

Shan fidgeted on the chair. "Maybe we ought to ride out a ways and meet them."

"They'll be along," Otto said, reaching for the jug, pouring amber liquid into his glass. "You know, after we take those heifers up there, you'll have to watch them pretty close. Some will try to come back home."

"I'll watch."

"If you get into trouble with them . . . if some of them don't calve-out right, saddle up and come get me."

"I will."

Otto drank, put the glass down, and breathed out. His eyes watered. "This last jug isn't as good as the others were," he said, looking at it.

"It tastes good to me, especially after the trouble." Otto was silent and Shan looked over at him. "Hadn't we better go down to Tico and tell the law what happened?"

"I'll do that. It was a fair fight, no one'll say much. They rode into the yard and tried to kill you in your own barn. A deputy'll probably ride up and ask you about it, that's about all. You just tell the truth, show him those stains on the spring box. I don't expect anything'll come of it. Wyoming law's pretty strong about a man having the right to protect his home and all." Otto pushed his glass away. "The thing that bothers me's how your wife's going to feel. I don't think they have many killings over in Nebraska any more."

"Yeah, I won't say much to her about it. Maybe I won't have to say anything, if you don't."

"Me?" Otto said. "I never talk about those things to anyone. Less said about those things the better. Of course she'll hear about it one way or another, but it won't come from me." Otto arose, went to the lamp, lit it, and straightened up, listening. "Sounds like a wagon coming." He was motionless a moment longer. "It is a wagon, come on."

They were out by the barn when Mrs. Muller wheeled in. Shan caught Sarahlee around the middle and lifted her down, drew her up against him in a bear hug. Her smiling mouth twisted a little in pain. He slacked off suddenly, staring at her—it was like in the dream. Then it passed and he crushed his mouth over hers, held her until she pushed against him. Her dark eyes glowed, laughed up into his face.

"It's seemed like ten years," he said.

149

She patted his cheek. "I missed you, too, Shan."

"Hey, Mary, hand me that big box and you take the other ones," Shan said.

Sarahlee watched Shan's big shoulders sag under the weight, and when he turned, straining, and asked what was in it, she laughed and said things for the cabin.

"Wedding presents from my family."

"Must be made of lead," he said. "How is your paw?"

"He's all right now."

Shan heard Mrs. Muller speak to Otto and listened. Her voice was low. "Did you get the hay hauled up to Shan's?"

"Well, no," Otto replied. "We thought we'd better ride up first and sort of look around."

"Are you still going to take the cattle up tomorrow?"

"We figure to, yes." Otto was throwing harness across the hitch rail when Mrs. Muller spoke again.

"What did you do up there?"

He looked at her. "Do? Why I just told you, Georgia."

She pointed. "You've got your pistol on, Otto."

Shan spoke swiftly. "Wolves, Missus Muller. Otto thought we'd better check on the wolves before we took the heifers up there to calve."

"Oh. Well, let's go inside. Mary, never mind those things, the men will fetch them."

Sarahlee touched Shan's arm, patted, and

150

squeezed it. "You need another haircut," she said.

He wanted to kiss her mouth again but Otto called to him. "Give me a hand here, Shan!"

They stood by the wagon until the women were down at the back door, then Otto spoke without looking at Shan. "I couldn't think what to say."

"I knew it when I looked at your face."

They unloaded the wagon, put Sarahlee's boxes under cannon cloth, and trudged down to the house. Inside, it was bright and coming alive with smells of cooking. Shan realized suddenly how hungry he was. Sarahlee was coatless and hatless and helping Mrs. Muller. Shan noticed a dimple in her elbow and marveled at it. He and Otto had another cupful of whiskey, then Otto put the jug in the corner near his rifle. Mary set the table and did not look at Shan.

"What'd your folks say when you told them you were married? I'll bet they near fainted."

"I didn't tell them until my father got better. My mother cried at first. She said Wyoming was so far off. My sister made me promise to send a picture of you." She looked around at him and smiled. "They want us to come back for a visit this fall."

Shan felt warm all over. "You ought to see our new barn. It's finished and it's bigger than the other one. You never saw such a barn in your life, Sarahlee. If it hadn't been for Otto, I don't know what we'd have done."

Mrs. Muller began taking bowls and platters

151

from the stove to the table. She looked inquiringly at her husband for a moment, then turned back and spoke to Sarahlee. "They've been sitting around here all afternoon drinking. I can tell. Otto doesn't like guns. When he's been drinking a lot, he gets absent-minded." She pointed to the pistol at her husband's side. "When he comes in, if he's wearing a gun, he always takes it off."

Sarahlee threw Otto a little smile and said nothing. Mary, in the background, looked from Otto to Shan and back again. There was no smile in her eyes. Otto got up and removed the shell belt and pistol, put them on the floor in the corner near the rifle, and went back to the table without a word.

At supper the conversation went in spurts. When the meal was over, Mrs. Muller said: "Take her for a walk, Shan. It's nearly full moon tonight. Mary and I'll clean up."

Otto arose. "I'll help," he said, and moved restlessly away from the table.

Shan took Sarahlee up the dusty path toward the barn. Habit made him pick the route. She was perfectly at ease, her stride nearly as long as his. When he leaned upon the hitch rail with the silver moon glowing through a curl-edged ring around it as large as a continent, she stood sideways, gazing at him.

"I have so much to tell you, Shan. The trip was hot, and after I got home I was so tired. . . ." She reached up and touched his hair, smoothed it back. "Georgia told me about Mary and those other Indians."

She looked more beautiful than ever in the soft, sad light, and when she mentioned the Indians, he stirred, shuffled his feet until he was closer to her.

"It was a tragic thing, Shan."

"Yes."

"But I understand how you felt about losing the barn."

He squirmed again, saying nothing and watching the moon.

"We should try to find out about Mary's kinsmen, though, don't you think? If she has parents, they must be sick over losing her."

"Sure," he said. "Come on, let's take a walk."

They went down across the milky land behind Otto's barn, holding hands, and he didn't stop until the lamplight from the house was almost indistinct, then he drew her up close and held her. She reached up, took his head in both hands, and held it so that he had to look into her eyes.

"I missed you more than I expected I would, Shan."

"Me, too. I'd think about you, picture you around the cabin. It was torture, Sarahlee."

She patted his cheek. "Well, I'm back and we'll make up for the past. We'll make everything like it should be, won't we?"

He strained against her, locked his mouth over her lips, and moved them, savoring the taste. She responded, but after a moment she pushed him back.

"Georgia told me about a school for Indians over in Colorado somewhere. Don't you think we ought to send Mary there? She could learn to be civilized."

"Sure." He let his arms drop down. "The only reason I've kept her this long was because I thought you might want to keep her. She could be a lot of help around the ranch."

"Like a slave?"

He shrugged. "We'd take care of her, give her clothes and things like that."

Her face clouded. "I don't understand you, Shan. Did you fight to free slaves?"

He laughed shortly. "Is that what I fought for?"

She took his hand and patted it, turned, and began to lead him back toward the house. "Let's go to bed, Shan, I'm tired. We've got a long time to talk about Mary and all those other things."

CHAPTER THIRTEEN

The following morning, bright and early, Mrs. Muller and Mary helped Otto re-load the wagon and hitch the team to it. When Shan and Sarahlee came out, Otto hiked for the barn to saddle two horses, then he waited inside the barn until Shan appeared in the doorway.

"Here," he said, blank-faced, "you ride this one and go open the gate on the heifers. I'll cut around through the feed lot and start them north."

The wagon was leaving the yard when they got the cattle lined out. For a while there was nothing to do but watch, then a few tried to cut back, but Otto's wise old bay horse always managed to anticipate them. But before they neared Shan's place, they were compelled to do a lot of extra riding. Because of this and the naturally slow pace, the women were already at the cabin and had a big meal prepared. Shan and Otto ate, then went back for a jag of hay. By the time they got back, night was falling. Otto borrowed the buggy to drive home in, and Shan left the wagon snugged up beside the barn. He meant to fork the hay in the next day.

When he finally washed up and entered the cabin, it was pitch dark out, the moon not yet risen. Sarahlee acted nervous toward him. She laughed aloud more than he'd ever seen her do before, and finally she took him outside, said he really ought to sleep in the yard or the barn because it wasn't decent, them sleeping in the cabin with Mary there. He was too weary to argue and took a large piece of cannon cloth, climbed up onto the wagonload of hay, and got comfortable. It was a wonderfully warm night and later, after the moon came up with a slice off the bottom of it, he studied the sky, noticed the wealth of humidity in the air, the mist over the stars. Then he slept.

It was almost 10:00 a.m. before Otto and Mrs. Muller drove up the next morning in Sarahlee's top buggy. They all had a cup of coffee before the men unloaded the hay and drove down to the Muller place for more, brought it back, unloaded it over the first pile, and leaned upon their forks, admiring the huge mound it made. They were both dark with sweat. Shan went to the spring box and sluiced off his upper body. Otto drank sparingly, then they saddled up and rode out to check the heifers.

"Don't look like any went back," Otto said.

"They're sure scattered out though."

"Fine feed up here. Well, let's get back. I expect the women'll have dinner ready."

They ate, and Sarahlee's face was flushed and shiny from the heat. Shan tried to keep from staring, but couldn't. She'd put away her heavier blouse, wore the thin white one he remembered. The swish of her long skirt made his flesh crawl. After the meal he went down by the spring box and looked down into the clear water. The dusted-over gouge was there to remind him of the fight. He bent down, made some mud of dust and water, and plastered it over the gouge, smoothed it out with his fingers. Otto walked up, smoking his pipe. He looked at the damp mud but said nothing about it. His face was red and weathered from the eyes down. From the eyes up it was almost indecently white where his hat had protected it.

"Hot, Shan," he said, looking out over the shimmering land. His whole face seemed to gather into vertical wrinkles up around his eyes, almost hiding them. "If I was a praying man, I'd get right down here in the mud and pray for rain."

"It's beginning to feel like rain," Shan said, and got up off his knees, looking toward the cabin. "What I need right now is a drink of whiskey."

"Go get the jug from under the bed. This is a nice cool place to enjoy a drink."

"You go get it."

Otto looked at him a moment, then chuckled and started back across the yard.

The day looked faded, tarnished. Shan squinted his eyes like Otto had done and squinted far out at the cattle. There were a few grazing in close, looking ungainly, all heavy with calf. He turned a little and looked up the north slope, wondered if Art Blessing's wife had come back, or if he'd died with his eyes closed and his back up against the old warped siding.

Otto came back with the jug. They sat down and took turns pulling at it for a while, then Otto scooped out a place in the mud and sunk it there to keep it cool.

"I've been thinking about the Blessings," Shan said. "We ought to ride over and see if that lady came back or not."

"Later," Otto said, "after it cools off a little."

Shan felt like there was lava bubbling in his blood. He filled his pipe and leaned back against the spring box, looking at Otto. "You seen other fights out here, Otto?"

"I've seen a few, yes. Let's forget that. Does no good to keep coming back to it, son."

"I guess not."

When daylight was fading, Otto, who was facing toward the cabin, smiled. "They've got tidies up over the windows," he said. "A man's house ought to look like women live in it, Shan."

Shan jumped up. "Come on, let's ride over and see what happened to Blessing."

They rode slowly, side-by-side, and with a rind of daylight holding fast off in the west just above the horizon. Otto's little eyes roved constantly, never stopping. "Time for the dogs to commence barking," he said when they broke over the ridge and began the descent. No dogs showed themselves or barked. Otto drew back on his reins. "Hold up a minute. It's awful quiet down there."

Shan stopped and bent forward a little. When he spoke, the words carried, bounced off the walls of the silent buildings. "They're gone off the porch."

Otto eased his horse out and Shan moved beside him. "Look there. That's where one of them is. That's Amos over there."

It was a freshly rounded grave, and although the newly moved earth was dry and cracking, it hadn't begun to settle yet. The grave wasn't more than a day old.

Otto stopped again and was motionless while he studied the house, the barn, and outbuildings. Nothing moved or made a sound. He moved out again, rode across in front of the house, and peered down at the headboard.

Amos Blessing
1835-1867

They rode back to the house and sat their saddles uncertainly, then Otto got down stiffly and went up under the overhang, and looked at the ground. "Bloodstains're still here," he said, then tried the door, flung it wide open. A squeaking echo went through the dingy rooms.

Shan dismounted and tied the horses, went over by the dug well, and drew up a bucket, drank from a rusty dipper, and refilled it for Otto. They stood by the well box, feeling uncomfortable.

"Let's go," Otto said finally, and didn't look back until they were upon the far ridge. "She must've been down there somewhere when we took them back, Shan. Hiding, I expect. Well, wherever Art is, he isn't going to use that fast gun any more."

They started down the southern slope and Otto looked far out. "Let's make a circle around the heifers before we ride back," he said.

They headed for one particular little herd of cattle standing close together, facing inward with the dying red sun slanting across their backs.

"They look like a sewing circle, don't they?" Otto said.

"What're they doing?"

"Come over here and you can see. One of them's having her calf."

Shan rode closer and stood in the stirrups. It thrilled him. The first calf born on his ranch—his and Sarahlee's ranch. At sight of them the little herd broke up, moved away a little. The mother cow stood up, facing them, shook her head in warning.

"I expect I've seen that happen a million times," Otto said, "but it makes me feel good every time I see it."

"It's sure little," Shan said, gazing at the dark, wet, curly object in the grass, then he transferred his attention to the cow. "She didn't have any trouble, Otto."

"No, most of them don't. Maybe I talked too much about that. I just wanted you to understand that with first-calf heifers you've got to watch them close while they're calving. Old cows don't have any trouble. It's just an occasional first-timer."

They lingered for a while, then headed for the barnyard. While they were unsaddling, Shan moved around so he could look up toward the cabin. Sarahlee was standing in the dooryard, peering down toward the barn, the sun behind her. It limned her. He stood there, staring, until Otto came up beside him, then they went to the house as Sarahlee headed inside. Right in front, where the sun hadn't been for a couple of hours, it was shady and pleasant. They both sank down and leaned back. Sarahlee came back out with a plate holding hot, fresh bread on it. A heavy wave of chestnut hair hung low over her forehead and her eyes sparkled at them. Otto joked with her about learning to cook.

"I know how to cook," she said, looking at Shan. "I've been cooking for ten years."

Otto got a twinkle in his eyes. "Sarahlee," he said slowly, "most womenfolk don't talk in years."

She laughed, and Shan smiled up at her. Mrs. Muller came out. Her cheeks were flushed and damp. "There's enough bread here to last two weeks," she said, then looked closely at her husband and lowered her voice. "You need a bath, Otto."

Sarahlee leaned beside Shan, touched his head, ran her fingers down along his neck, and caught at the thick skin inside his collar, and kneaded it. He got covered with little tiny bumps.

"You, too, Shan."

"All right. Get me the lye soap."

They went down to the spring box behind the

161

barn. Otto had an odd way of bathing. He stripped from the waist down first, scrubbed himself, then put on his underpants and trousers and removed his upper clothing, washed that part of his body, then re-dressed.

It was growing dark by the time they returned to the cabin. A lamp was burning inside on the table. The women had also hung another lamp from the ceiling and to one side of the stove. When Shan entered ahead of Otto, Mary threw him a quick look from the dishpan, then went on scrubbing something furiously.

Supper was pleasant and gay. Mrs. Muller took more liberties with Shan than she ever had before, and it rather embarrassed him. Otto went back down to the spring box, dug the rye jug out, and brought it back, poured two cups full, and toasted the new house. Later, he and Otto went back outside. It seemed that as large as the cabin was, it was too small for five people. They sat on the ground with the sounds from within making a background to their thoughts. After a while Otto said: "This is what it's like, Shan. Multiply this a thousand times, maybe a million times, and you'll know what your evenings are going to be like from now on. Someday you'll have a floor in the cabin, maybe another room or two, and likely a covered porch, but those sounds will always be pretty much the same. A cow bawling out there in the dark, a horse cribbing on the manger in the barn. Woman talk, summer nights. Woman talk, winter nights. Bad winters, drought, death come on your range, different kinds of troubles, but the evenings will be about like this one tonight. You like it?"

"I like it all right, Otto."

A little later Mrs. Muller went past them in the gloom. They watched her head for the barn. When she returned, she smiled, passed them, and reëntered the cabin. A few moments later Sarahlee came out, heading the same way. Shan watched the roll of her movement, the way she carried her head. When she, too, came back, he was filling his pipe. She reached over and touched him, then disappeared inside. He squirmed on the ground and Otto spoke softly without looking around.

"Just one more night, son, then Georgia and I'll be going home."

They called out their good nights and went toward the barn, burrowed into the hay, and lay back. Otto squinted at the sky a while, then averted his face, but Shan looked steadily upward. Little lanterns flickered up there. When the moon arose much later, he noticed the slice off the bottom now extended part way up the side. Clean, he thought, clean as ice. Rides alone up there and doesn't see a single thing. Doesn't hear anything or smell anything. A man could lie in the hay until Dooms- day with a fire in his guts like hot shot and that big ball of nothing would never know he was alive.

He turned upon his side and gazed down across the land. It was too quiet. The cattle were still and no coyotes sounded. Beyond, he could see Otto's form, broad and flat in slumber. His right arm was flung out, fingers partially hooked, fingers that had sent a big rifle ball through a man's brain. Fingers turned to soft silver by moonlight. Dead fingers like Amos Blessing was dead. Art Blessing . . . ruined. Unable to hold a pitchfork again, an axe, a saddle horn . . . a gun. He stirred and looked out where the ground swelled upward into the dividing, long slope of land. What about the woman? Cried, sure, cried buckets full when she'd come creeping out of hiding and found the inert bodies, one dead, one near death.

What would become of the Blessing Ranch— the land, cattle, horses? There were Blessing animals strung out far and wide—who would get them now? Excitement swept up through him. He raised up on one arm, looking down into the yard by the spring box. Otto would know what was right, but one thing was sure. Shan was in the best possible position to profit from unbranded Blessing calves, and this was calving time. Blessing calves, enough of them to fill his corrals. More than he'd get from his share of the Muller calves. Instead of waiting out a lean five years to get into the cattle business, he could do it in one year.

A phantom slipped out of the shadows by the

cabin. It took a moment for his mind to attach significance to it, then he watched, focused his eyes, closed his mind down around its progress across the yard. It was Mary. He could see her better after she moved out into the moonlight. She was making for the barn. He watched until she disappeared from view. She was carrying something. What was she up to? He drew his legs up cautiously, moved clear of the hay, and worked his way toward the loft ladder, went down it a rung at a time until he was just inside the door, where he flattened, listening. There wasn't a sound. He eased outside into the shadows of the building and made his way stealthily toward the corner. His heart was thudding by the time he got close enough to see her.

There was something holding her hair back so that it fell around her shoulders as black as coal except where the silver light shone down upon it. She was taking a bath at the spring box with her back to him. He watched, feeling ashamed, and when she drew up, dry, and threw her head back to look up into the bowl of heaven, there was sweat running down his chest and in the palms of his hands. He thought she was like a doe, built to run, to watch, to fade into shadows. She was symmetrical, beautifully light, and frail-appearing. There was nothing sturdy or heavy about her.

"Mary. . . ."

She moved so swiftly, for a second he lost her

in the gloom by the spring box. He moved forward, and when she arose from behind the logs, she had the gingham dress on. She didn't run or speak angrily or, as he'd done, throw a clod at him. She just stood there, watching him come closer.

The pine needles and sweet-grass scents were mixed with the less attractive and sterile odor of lye soap. When he stopped, looking down into her face, he couldn't think of a single appropriate word to say. He reached out and touched her with one large hand. Let the fingers lie lightly on her shoulder. She was like a soft bronze statue in the moon's flat rays. Behind them was the ghostly outline of buildings, forgotten now.

"Let's walk," he said. "Come on."

They went east. The barn lay between them and the cabin. Shan thought it was like being drunk, what he was doing. You knew, you knew perfectly well, but you went ahead anyway. He stepped on a cocklebur with his bare foot, stopped, swore softly, and pulled the thing out, and resumed his way without looking around at her. Walked until a little blur of dark shadow turned out to be a clump of scrub oak, lithe and beautiful in the strange, hushed world of night, and there he stopped.

She stood beside him, and at first she didn't look at anything else but his bigness, the broad sweep of chest, the pale flow and ripple of muscle when he moved. The strange little thing in the side of his cheek that jerked.

She turned a little to see the land, the clear, crystal sky, blue-gray with a ragged fringe of dirty old silver far out along the horizon. The silence everywhere, deep and lasting.

"You like me, Mary?"

She nodded, still solemnly looking beyond, far out, into eternity.

He touched her again, caught her in both arms, and drew her close. She neither responded nor resisted, and he loosened his hold. Then she did an unexpected thing; she put her hands up to his face and held it averted, away from her, and studied it. He forced his head back around and bent forward. Her hands went down to his waist and hung on. Where the fingers lay, widespread, it burned like hot iron.

He kissed her. It was like drawing something out of himself, something savage to match her own ferocity, and he moved back afterward.

"Sit down."

She sat, face away from him. "You good man, Shan. Strong man." Then she turned suddenly and smiled, and all the impassivity she was capable of disappeared forever between them. The moon made her golden-colored. Black eyes as deep as night clung to him. He dropped down unsteadily upon the warm earth.

"Those Indians you killed . . ."

"What about them?"

"They make me go. They stoled me."

"Stole you? Why, I thought one of them was your husband, Mary . . . or maybe your brother."

She shook her head shortly. "Stole me to take far away. No good."

"What were they doing at my ranch?"

"See smoke before sunup, ride over. Not long you come, big fight, run, run . . ." She leaned toward him. "You want to kill me, too?"

He flushed. "I thought you were a buck Indian then. I didn't know you weren't until I shot your horse, Mary."

She continued to bend toward him, stare into his eyes. "You like me, Shan?"

He made no answer. A hotness was engulfing him, flooding upward inside his head. She bent closer, touched him with a small hand, dropped her head swiftly and pecked at his mouth, drew back, and made a gentle, strange smile. His heart was pounding.

She leaned over him and trilled a song. There were no words and the music was more chant than song, but the movements that went with it left little to be imagined about its purpose and meaning, and in the end, because passion was beyond prudence and her deep nature in all its simplicity invited it, they were close. A half of him was placid and filled with a richness, the other half was suffocated and lost.

CHAPTER FOURTEEN

The next morning it rained. Shan had ridden out before daybreak and wasn't there for breakfast. As soon as he had eaten, Otto also saddled up and rode out among the cattle. When he found Shan, standing beside his dark-wet horse in the downpour, he laughed at him, his face shiny with water.

"Now the feed'll last," Otto said over the splash and hiss of water. "I could get down and wallow in it. There'll be plenty of hay, too, son. This is the prettiest thing I've seen this year, this rain water."

Shan looked up at him, his unruly hair plastered flat. "How'll that little calf make out?"

"Hah! As long as they get a gut full of warm milk first, they can make it through a blizzard. A little rain don't hurt them." Otto gestured with a dripping shirt sleeve where the cattle were standing humped up with their rumps to the north against the force of the storm. "They'll drift with it. You'll have to ride a little and haze them back to your range, but rain water never hurt them. Never at all." He dropped his arm. "I guess that's what you figured, why you came out here so early. They're holding breakfast for you. Let's go back."

Shan looked at the fish-belly sky a moment. Off in the east were some monstrous old thunderheads. They reminded him of the greasy smoke that rises above burning towns. He turned swiftly and mounted, settled into the saddle. "I could use some hot coffee," he said.

They turned, rode toward the glistening barn, and Otto talked most of the way back. Shan's head was down, rain water running in a dirty trickle off his black hat.

When they put up the horses, Otto stood in the drafty doorway, admiring the sullen sky. "Not everyone that comes out here gets a good summer, boy. You're lucky." Shan fiddled with the saddle, finally hung it up, and went back to look at his horse. He seemed in no hurry to go to the cabin. "We'll have fat cattle to sell this fall," Otto went on. "This is a lucky year."

Shan finally went to the door and looked out. Up the slope where he'd been the night before by the clump of scrub oak were some cattle. "Otto," he said flatly, "what'll happen to the Blessing range and cattle?"

Otto's expansive smile dimmed a little. He looked at Shan's solemn profile. "The range'll be open for public use, I expect, unless they've got an heir to come out here and take it up. The cattle . . . well, they'll have calves just like they've always done."

"I know."

Otto walked heavily out into the mud, hesitated, and looked back. "How many calves would you say it would take to replace a burned-out barn?" He started forward. "Come on, we can lace that coffee with your rye whiskey."

Shan forced himself out into the yard, felt the quick, driving lash of rain across his shoulders, kept his head down until they were at the door, then he raised it. Mrs. Muller was smiling at Otto. Sarahlee swept up and laughed at Shan.

"You must have been a long way out when it started."

"I was."

"You'd better get into dry clothing or you'll catch your death of colic, Shan."

He saw Mary's black eyes on him and turned away from her. The Mullers were more than happy over the rain; they were unusually gay. Mrs. Muller helped Shan rig up a blanket-partition for him to change his clothes behind, and afterward they ate another breakfast, all of them. Otto laced the coffee, even for the women. They sat inside with the cabin door open, looking out, listening to the drum roll across the shake roof and talking over the racket it made. Finally Otto got up.

"We'd better head back, Georgia," he said. "Shan, how about me taking the buggy and riding back, when this lets up, for the team and wagon?"

"Sure, Otto. Sarahlee and I'll bring the team and wagon down the next day or two. You don't have to make the extra trip."

After the Mullers left, waving and smiling through the drenching, Sarahlee put a shawl over her head and shoulders and went down to the barn with Shan while he fed the stock. She walked through the building, touching things, breathing deeply of the wet fragrance.

"It smells so good in here, Shan."

"Yeah." Somewhere north of the barn a cow bawled and another one answered her. He poked his head out the doorway and listened. Sarahlee came up behind him, brushed against him.

"Could it be another calf, Shan?"

He gripped the door post with one hand when he answered. "It might be. I expect I ought to go look."

She reached up and pushed that hanging lock of hair away from his forehead. "If you must," she said. "I'll give you another haircut tonight." Her voice was deep and tender. "You're as shaggy as a bear."

He watched her walk through the mud toward the cabin, holding up her skirt, then he re-saddled and rode out into the rain, went north toward the slope. He found no calf nor even a calfy heifer, and now the water was cold, chilling, so he turned and went back, put up the horse, and stood in the barn entrance smoking his pipe and listening soberly to the gush of water for a long time before squashing through the mud to the cabin.

He put on more dry clothes behind the blanket

partition and sat on a chair, looking outside, while Sarahlee and Mary made supper. The rain never slackened. It beat on the roof all night long and drowned out everything else.

When they retired, he left the partition to Sarahlee first. When she called, low, he got up and undressed behind it. Mary was on the other side on her pallet. Sarahlee had blown the lamp out, and when he got in next to her in the Stygian darkness, he was trembling. When she lay as still as he did, he was thankful. Just before he fell asleep she reached over, pulled him close to her, and stroked his face, patted his hair back, and rocked him in her arms in the gentlest way, making everything seem right, all the shame and guilt flowing out of him. He fell asleep.

Just as Otto had wished, the rain kept up for two days. Shan rode out in it on the second day, but he wore a gum coat, so that when he got back to the barn he was dry. Sarahlee made him leave his boots just inside the doorway and walk around in his stocking feet. After the boots got warm, they smelled like the corral, so she had Mary put rags over them.

That second night was better. When Sarahlee went behind the curtain, he was left by the table with his coffee. He heard Mary behind him, busy by the stove. Her normally quiet movements were loud to him. Passing, she touched the back of his head. When he looked up, she smiled at him.

Later, when he retired, Sarahlee cradled his head again as though he were a little boy. The coyotes came back and started their sounding at the dying moon.

When he went outside to feed the following morning, the sun was up with a vengeance. Earth steamed, the air was so clear he could see details along the north ridge. Later, when he rode out, sunlight flooded everything, relaxed him with its warmth, made him all loose inside.

The heifers were separating into little cliques. Some had found Blessing cows to herd with, and these he looked at closely. Some were bumping big calves, waddled when they walked.

He rode farther out than he'd ever ridden before. Out where there were gullies deep enough to lose a horse in, and more rolling country with greater clumps of trees northeast. He saw tiers of forest like stair steps, marching one after another up the sides of fat, round mountains. He dismounted by a brawling little creek, let the horse drag his reins, and graze. He made a cigarette and lit it. He sat there, near some ancient teepee rings, feeling warm. When it got hotter, steamingly humid and energy-draining, he lay on his side, smoking, looking west. The sun kept getting hotter, the air heavier and harder to breathe like it was soupy and leaden, and when he got too drowsy to resist it, he stumped out the cigarette, lay back full length, and slept.

He dreamed of the old woman first. She was stroking his forehead like she had done, then she took her hand away, drew up very straight, and shook her head at him. The sense of guilt swept over him, stronger than ever, and he rolled over in his sleep. The grass tickled his cheek, made him dream of Sarahlee stroking his face. Sarahlee raised up slowly and stopped stroking, and leaned over looking down at him, but she didn't shake her head, she looked sad for him. Not angry or outraged or disapproving, just sad for him like a mother would be.

She raised up straighter. He was looking up at her. Where her bosom jutted so big, he couldn't see her mouth or nose, but her eyes were clear to him and they were soft, darkly pitying. She was something . . . something . . . strength. Sarahlee was strength. . . .

The horse nickering awakened him. He got up swiftly and felt instinctively for the butt of his pistol. The fogginess of confused dreaming clutched his mind; it required a real struggle to clear it. There was nothing to see, although he swung his head, heard the dull roll of his beating heart. The horse was eating again. He lay back down on his stomach, propped his chin on one palm, and studied the countryside minutely. It wasn't likely there was trouble around, but he knew better than to ignore any warning, no matter how unseemly. Later, satisfied he was alone and unobserved, he lay back and closed his eyes again. After a while his back began to ache and he awakened again, got up and stretched, flicked sweat off his face, went to the creek to wash the sour taste from his mouth, then made another cigarette, and just stood there, wide-legged, big, and ramrod-straight, smoking.

Clouds, horizontal strings of bulky yarn, fuzzy and purest white, were strung across the sky. The sun shimmered; it was hot. At his feet pressed-down grass whispered and rustled. He could almost see it growing. That had been a godsend, that rain.

He mounted and started back. Once in a while he'd run across little bunches of cattle. Twice he found new calves, and both times they were with Blessing cows. He was tempted but didn't catch and mark them. There was plenty of time yet. If someone rode along and found calves with his brand sucking Blessing cows, they'd know what he had done. Later, when they were four or five months old, it would be better; they'd be about weaned by then.

He thought of that while the horse picked its languid way down to familiar country. When it was safe, he'd brand some of those calves, take payment for the burned barn like Otto had said. A couple dozen calves maybe, fifty or sixty, he'd see when the time came. The important thing was to be first. Otto wouldn't bother, he knew, but those O'Briens might, or their riders. Cowboys with a yen to start out were notoriously handy with lariats. He smashed out a cigarette on the saddle horn and tossed it away. Far out, glimmering in the sparkling light, was his barn. It jutted, big and square. He was filled with pride. Beyond it was the cabin, not so handsome but drawing him.

When he got to the barn, the daylight was softening, the sun sinking in the west. He went in and ate. There were crickets singing in the dusty yard beyond, a strong scent from some acid weed in the heavy night air. He thought of what Otto had said about the evenings being like this for the rest of his life. An uneasiness stirred in him.

For the next three days he was busy with the cattle, and meanwhile Sarahlee and Mary worked at making a home, at provisioning it with glassed goods on shelves. Mary could carry on a running conversation and she would laugh with Sarahlee and even tease Shan a little, now and then, like Sarahlee did. Then Sarahlee decided she would drive her yellow-wheeled buggy down to the Mullers. While she was telling Shan, he could see Mary's face over her shoulder, the black eyes full on him.

"Will you hitch up for me, Shan?"

"Sure."

He went to the barn, harnessed the mare, and

put her between the shafts. His heart was beating strongly, the sense of guilt coming and going like fever. When Sarahlee came out, he was busy picking chaff out of the mare's mane.

"Can you come along, Shan? Otto's always so glad to see you?"

He shook his head, bent low while he adjusted a buckle. "Next time maybe. Tell Otto the heifers are calving out good but he was right about them keeping a man busy." He stepped back and smiled at her. "If Otto's got an extra jug, ask him if he'll sell it to you."

She said yes, she would, threw him a smile, and drove across the yard. He stood just inside the barn with the coolness on him and his heart beating like a trip hammer until the buggy was a speck southward, then he went as far as the bench he'd built beside the cabin door and sank down.

"Shan?"

He made no answer and sweat dappled his face. The land was shimmering more than usual. The yarn clouds had broken up, become feathery-looking and graceful. They scarcely moved at all. Mare's-tails folks called clouds like that. . . .

"Shan?"

He got up. When she came out, moving slowly, he looked down at her. The black eyes were shiny and she wore a yellow dress Sarahlee had made for her. It fitted better than the gingham one, and when she moved, there wasn't a ripple, just flowing movement. Watching her with his mind, feeling drunk without being drunk, a recollection came back. It had been after the fight at Sailor's Creek and all the exhausted soldiers were sprawled and numb and silent. The chaplain had stopped to speak. He had said: "Men are part of the dust and the earth . . . they were created to struggle." Created to struggle! Look at her! You couldn't put your head in the soft place of her shoulder and feel the shame dissolve; there was no soft place. She was different, totally different, from Sarahlee. She made you feel so damned big and powerful, so—created to struggle, so willing. . . .

"Do you want to go for a ride, Mary?"

"Yes."

"Come on."

They went down to the barn, got two horses, and rode. They covered aimless hot miles, seeking shade and coolness. It happened often after that. Whenever Sarahlee went down to the Mullers', they rode the range with the hot summer, golden and dancing around them. She would laugh with him and hold his hand and ride close so that their legs bumped. Other times she'd bend over and break away on her horse, and when he'd come thundering up, she wouldn't be sitting there waiting for him, she'd be under a tree or on a shady slope with a buck brush hedge all around, and he'd get down all prickly with heat.

Then the cows seemed to all start calving at the

same time, and he had very few minutes with either Mary or Sarahlee for days at a time. He would come in late at night, wash off at the spring box, trudge to the cabin and eat, drop to sleep almost before he went to bed. It thinned him down to sinew and bone.

Then one time he was over east of the road, driving back seven head with calves by their sides, when he saw a rider coming. He thought it was Otto so he shooed the cows onto his own range, drew up, and waited. But it was a stranger with a slow smile, a big frame, and a sidearm held flat to his right leg by a thong. When they were close, the stranger asked Shan who he was. When Shan told him, he answered with that slow, disarming grin, and Shan's stomach tightened. Among the seven cows were several Blessing animals with his iron on them.

"I seen Otto in town a week or so back," the stranger said. "He told me about the fight at your place."

"Oh. Well, let's get out of the sun."

They rode on over to Shan's barn and dismounted. The lawman tied his horse and crossed the yard at Shan's invitation. He introduced the deputy marshal to Sarahlee and Mary. His wife said they would eat soon and it would be a pleasure to have the deputy marshal stay. He thanked her with old-fashioned courtesy and went back outside with Shan.

The jug Sarahlee had brought back from Otto's was under the bench, wrapped with sacking, the whiskey cool. Shan wiped off the mouthpiece and handed it to the deputy. He drank deeply.

"My wife knows nothing about that," Shan said. "You see, she's from the settlements and I figured it'd upset her."

"Sure, I understand. Tell me your side of it."

Shan told him. They went to the spring box, looked at the bullet gouge, the fading stain, then went around back where Amos Blessing had died. After a while they sat in the shade of the barn and the lawman smoked.

"That's about like Otto told it," he said. "It's no loss. Art and Amos were always stirring up trouble." He looked around. "You've sure done a lot of work out here, Mister Shanley." His lean, bronzed face creased into a soft smile. "I reckon the Blessings bit the wrong wolf this time."

"After we left them on the porch," Shan said, "we got to worrying about the wounded one and rode back. There was a new grave north of the house but the other one . . . Art . . . was gone. All the horses and dogs were gone, too. I've always wondered about that."

Sarahlee called from the cabin. The lawman unwound off the ground, dusted his britches off, and said: "Art died. His woman was taking him to the railhead in their wagon and he died. I don't know what became of her. Went back East, I reckon."

"Died?"

"He bled a barrel full, didn't he?"

"Yes, he bled a lot before Otto got it tied off."

"We better not keep your wife waiting."

They ate and shortly afterward the lawman said good bye and started back. It was a long ride, he said, and he didn't want to get back to Tico after midnight.

Later, when Shan was watering the horses, Sarahlee came out and wanted to know why he had stopped at their place.

"Just out riding around," Shan told her. "Getting acquainted. He'd heard we were up here and thought he ought to ride by."

She watched the horse drink. "My father said he'd help us if things were bad, Shan."

He looked at her. "Bad? What do you mean?"

"If we owed money we couldn't pay, things like that."

His face cleared. "Oh. Well, we don't owe anything, Sarahlee. I know we don't have much, but we don't owe anything on anything."

She looked relieved and changed the subject. "How do the cattle look?"

"Fine. I had seven cows with me when I met the marshal. That's where I'm going now. Want to get them back on our range before it gets too dark. I'll be a little late for supper I expect."

CHAPTER FIFTEEN

He rode steadily after that and almost every day he found new calves. Several times he had to use his rope and saddle horse to deliver a calf, and twice he found dead ones with frantic and bagged-up cows bawling over them. It made him resentful but he remembered what Otto had said —there would be some calves that would die or be born dead. So far, however, he had not lost a cow; he'd had to clean out a few, which was the job he cared least for, but he hadn't lost one. Later on he built a narrow chute in one corral where he'd drive the cows requiring cleaning out. That way, by blocking their hind legs so they couldn't kick, he was able to do a more thorough job. The cows were pretty wild and he learned how to avoid their heels and horns.

Three days after Sarahlee's last trip to the Mullers place he was riding a north ridge when he saw a rider approaching through the clumps of cattle southward. He drew up motionless, watching the horseman's progress. It appeared to him that the stranger was looking at brands, studying the condition of the cattle, and fear closed his throat momentarily. He loosened the pistol at his hip and zigzagged down the slope. When he got close, he recognized the nearly square form on the big bay horse. It was Otto.

Shan made no pretense when they reined up, looking at one another. "You gave me a bad few seconds, Otto."

Muller made a wry grin and looked at the nearest cattle. "I can see why," he said. "How many have you got so far?"

"Twenty-eight." The back of Shan's neck got red. "If I didn't, someone else would, wouldn't they?"

"Sure," Otto said easily. "You don't have to tell me how it is. I understand. How're the heifers coming?"

"Fine," Shan said, and told Otto about the stillborns, the abandoned calves, and the number he'd cleaned up.

"I've been riding through them," Otto said, "and they look better'n I expected. The last time Sarahlee was down she said you were riding from dawn till sundown. I thought I'd ride up and see if I could help you any."

They rode slowly toward the cabin and Shan gave him the figures, showed him the oldest calves and the newest ones. Otto reiterated satisfaction. "They're calved out enough so that you can take a day off now and then," he said. "Come down and visit when Sarahlee drives down. Georgia's been wondering why you haven't been down."

They dismounted at the barn. Shan looked across the saddle seat at Otto, but the older man was tying his horse, face averted.

"I'll do that, Otto. Next time we'll drive down together."

Otto turned and watched Shan unsaddle, turn his horse into a pole corral. "The hay crop looks good up here," he said, and turned to watch a ground-swelling breeze rustle through the tall grass running uphill. "We got to start cutting pretty quick now. You ever get that prairie meadow fenced?"

"Not yet, but I will."

"It don't matter," Otto said carelessly. "After that rain the cattle couldn't trample enough to hurt anyway. We've got to get it in before the autumn rains, though."

"I expect we can," Shan said, walking back out into the sunlight and following Otto's northward gaze. "Let's go see what's left in the jug." While they crossed the yard, he told Otto about the deputy marshal's visit and Otto nodded.

"He said he'd come up and talk to you, then, when he was riding back, he stopped for a minute at my place. He said he wasn't sorry the Blessings got it, Shan."

"That's all there is to it?"

"That's all. From now it's history and let's just forget it."

Sarahlee and Mary surprised them. They had the table set for four, had seen Shan and Otto riding up together. The meal was a pleasant one, and afterward Shan drove Otto out across the range in Sarahlee's top buggy, made a large curve east of the road into the regions Otto had not ridden. When they approached the tall, lonely tree under which Shan had cut the little Durham bull, they stopped to smoke and watch the long, lingering day come to a close.

"It looks like a ranch ought to look," Otto said. "It won't be long until it'll be paying you a living."

Overhead the shadowed sky was glowing red; it looked worn and faded far out where the sun's last reflections touched. The air smelled of heat still, leavened with the lessening of light but hot nevertheless. There was a great depth and a mellowness to the sunset. Objects were rounded and soft-looking.

"Sarahlee like it, Shan?"

"She likes it fine."

"And you? Had any doubts since we rebuilt the barn and she came back?"

Shan twisted on the seat to look at Otto. The older man was smoking his pipe placidly, face impassive. "No, I'm satisfied, Otto."

"Well, I expect that's more'n half the battle, son. There're other things, like the work, but you'd find them any place, and if a man's to get ahead, he's got to work hard wherever he puts down roots."

"Sure," Shan said.

"Decided yet what you're going to do with Mary? I expect she's a help to Sarahlee."

"She is. No, we haven't talked about it lately."

"Well," Otto said knocking out his pipe, "let's get back. I want to get home before dark."

They drove to the barn, and while Shan removed the buggy mare's harness, Otto saddled his horse. He bade Shan good bye at the barn and rode across the yard, bowed from the saddle when Sarahlee came to the door, and rode out west toward the road. Shan stood by the buggy, watching him go.

The day after Otto's visit Sarahlee and Mary worked on more preserves against the long winter. Sarahlee caught Shan at the barn and asked him if he'd go down to Tico for jars and sealing tops, sugar, alum, and salt. The following morning before dawn, Shan passed the Mullers place but didn't stop because he knew they weren't up yet. At Tico he found a bargain in two porkers and hauled them back alive. With Mary's aid he dressed them; afterward Sarahlee took over. She knew how to put down pork, which neither Shan nor Mary had ever done before. The cabin was laden with supplies. Too laden, Sarahlee said, and Shan undertook to build a spring house around the spring box. He had the water trenched to circulate and run under the plank flooring. The walls were insulated with tree bark until the temperature inside, when he finished, never varied summer or winter. It required five days to complete the spring house, then all three of them worked one whole morning, transferring the winter supplies from the cabin to its smooth new shelves.

After that, there were a few idle days and Shan got restless. He wondered when Otto would want to start haying. Occasionally Sarahlee would ride out with him when he checked the cattle, but they were almost all calved-out now, so they explored a little and once he took her to the brawling little creek where the Indian rings were. While they were there, he made love to her, and afterward he got the shakes and was angry at himself, smoked a cigarette, and said very little on the return trip until they were nearing the cabin, then he drew up, sat there, looking at the distant mountains turning soft red under a setting sun.

"It's beautiful, Sarahlee. See how those big damned mountains off there in the west sort of background the cabin and barn."

"It is beautiful," she said. Then: "Shan, you simply must stop swearing so much."

The next day they left Mary at the ranch and drove down in the top buggy to visit the Mullers. Mrs. Muller met them with an animated smile and inspected Shan closely, remarked that he looked thinner, that he probably was trying to do in one summer what he ought to spread out over five. Otto was out back, working on his haying tools, and came around the barn at the sound of voices with his shirt tail hanging out and his little pipe unlit and forgotten in his mouth. He stuffed the shirt in when he saw Sarahlee, waved back to her before she disappeared inside, and waited for Shan to walk up. Otto had a jug near the cotton-wood tree across the barnyard near his equipment shed. He beckoned Shan toward it, brought it out, and dusted it off.

"To haying time," he said, and held it out as Shan came close. "We've got to get started pretty quick."

Shan drank, and returned the jug. The whiskey made him breathe shallow for a moment and wag his head. "That's why I came down with Sarahlee today, to find out when you wanted to start."

"Well," Otto said, setting the jug aside, "we should have started a couple of weeks ago, but, by golly, I've had more riding to do this year than ever before."

"Why?"

"Too much feed. The cattle drift more. Every little creek's running full where most of them'd be dry this late in the year. The critters drift to Kingdom Come and back. And there's another thing, too. We've got more cattle on the range. They keep mixing up."

"O'Brien cattle?"

"Theirs, yes, but some new brands. Marks I've never seen before. I guess more settlers are coming in."

"I've seen brands I didn't recognize," Shan said,

"but it didn't mean much to me. The only ones I know are yours, O'Brien's, and Blessing's."

"Well, north of the old Blessing place there is the Monroe Ranch. The Weaver outfit is about twelve miles west of you. I know their marks, but there're new ones this year, too, brands I've never seen before. It's a good sign. The country's growing up."

From the back of the house came the insistent clamor of the supper triangle. Otto put the jug away and started down toward the house. Shan fell in beside him. At the washstand out back, Shan splashed water over his face. It felt refreshing as it dried on his skin. Otto dashed water over himself and blew through his fingers each time he did it. Then they went inside and took chairs at the table. The meal consisted mainly of fried chicken, which pleased Shan. He told Otto's wife he thought she was the only woman in Wyoming who knew how to fry a chicken right. It pleased her.

"We're going to crate up some hens and a rooster for you to take home," Mrs. Muller told him. "You need chickens up there."

"We don't have a place for them yet," Shan said.

Otto laughed. "You'll make a place. When your woman wants chickens, you'll make a place for them all right."

Mrs. Muller said: "You ought to have a milk cow, too."

Otto looked up with a sudden thought. "I've got a nice little brindle cow'll be coming fresh in a day or so, Shan. You can take her up there and milk her for her keep. I don't like milking two cows at a time unless I've got porkers, and those I don't have now. What do you say?"

It made no difference to Shan either way. Like all cattlemen, he was an indifferent milker. The responsibility of having to milk a cow twice a day didn't bother him because responsibility never had anyway. "Thanks, Otto," he said, "we'll take good care of her."

Mrs. Muller looked from Shan to her husband and back to Sarahlee. "When the child comes, you'll need lots of milk and cream," she said.

Otto's hand froze in mid-air. Shan's jaws locked in a bulging stillness. He raised his eyes to Mrs. Muller's face. Sarahlee was stirring her coffee, stopped, turned a burning brick red, and did not look up.

"She just told me."

Otto leaned back and looked at Shan, whose hands had begun to move along the edge of the table like crippled things. "Congratulations," Otto said, then got up, got the jug, and filled two glasses from it. "To a boy," he said lifting his glass. "Maybe twin boys."

When the meal was over, Shan paused a moment behind Sarahlee at the wash pan, put a hand on her shoulder, and squeezed gently, then he went on outside where Otto was waiting.

They sat in the shade at the side of the house, their talk desultory. Shan felt like he'd been kicked in the stomach by a mule.

Later, when he and Sarahlee were driving homeward, she told him how she hadn't been sure. How she'd wanted to talk to Mrs. Muller. It would be born in February. She and Mrs. Muller had figured it out. "I'll have to get some things, Shan. I'd like to take Mary and drive into Tico tomorrow, if it's all right."

"All right? Sure, Sarahlee, you do anything you want to do."

And that was one time he was glad Mary went away the same time Sarahlee did. He stood in the barn's shade, watching them drive off, then he saddled up and rode aimlessly northward. When he got to the sloping ridge between his range and the Blessing range, he sat up there for a while, until the sun grew hot, then he went along the rim as far as a clump of trees and laid down in the grass.

A man was supposed to be happy at this time, he knew, but he wasn't. He felt mixed up, bewildered, and fearful. He lay upon his back, looking up through the tree limbs at the flawless sky. In his mind he saw Sarahlee's handsome, still face, the soft shape of her shoulders, and the shining of her hair; he remembered the almost overwhelming warmth that had flowed over him from her, the way she had rocked him, crooned softly to him, winnowing out his earlier shame and guilt until his fierce desire had dwindled, had become, instead of an urge for mating, a need for mothering.

Later, he rode west across the road. He rode without purpose as though movement in itself was good, and when he saw the rider approaching in a shambling walk, he sat still, watching him. It was Ash O'Brien. He smiled through the tanned, lean strength of his face at Shan.

"Howdy, Mister Shanley."

"Just plain Shan. Howdy. How are your cattle doing?"

"Real well. How are yours doing?"

"The same. They're just about calved-out and I'm thankful for that."

Young O'Brien's blue eyes twinkled. "I know. I never cared for that end of the business, either. You got a lot of Blessing animals on your side of the road?"

"Quite a few, yes." Shan watched the younger man's face closely. "Have you?"

"Yes, and my paw don't know hardly what we ought to do with them."

"Well," Shan said, "if they're eating off your grass, why don't you push them off somewhere?"

"We do, but, hell, the next morning they're back. There's quite a few of them, too, a lot of unbranded calves, and that ain't very good for us."

"Why not?"

"Rustlers," O'Brien said. "If the news gets around, there'll be a long-rope artist behind every bush. As far as we're concerned, we don't care who brands them, but if rustlers get thick out here, we'll lose, too . . . and so will you and Otto and everybody else."

"I didn't think of that," Shan said.

"We're branding all our little calves as soon as we find them, but it makes a heap of extra riding." O'Brien sat slouched in the saddle. "We heard about those Indians burning your barn," he said.

Shan was watching his face, saw the way Ash O'Brien's eyes brightened in speculation. He shook his head at the younger man. "It wasn't the Indians. You know that, too."

O'Brien's quick grin came up. He looked a little embarrassed. "Well, we did hear later you found out it wasn't Indians, come to think of it."

"What'd you hear about the fight?"

"With the Indians?"

"With the Blessings."

"Funny how quick word gets around, ain't it? Oh, we heard there was a fight. The Blessings tried to bushwhack you in your new barn and got killed. Folks in Tico seem to think Art and Amos got what they'd been asking for."

Shan looked into the young face and saw nothing there but frankness. He pulled the reins through his fingers and snapped them a couple of times. "They'd ridden down a couple of times before, trying to pick a fight."

"That's the way they were. Our outfit always steered clear of them."

"Well," Shan said, "I expect I'd better head for home. My wife went to town. She'll need me to unload the buggy when she gets back."

"I saw her go past. Her and the Injun girl."

Shan rode homeward, feeling morose. He'd gotten two distinct impressions from his talk with O'Brien. One was about the Blessing cattle. Undoubtedly the O'Briens, doing extra riding like Ash had said, had come across some of the calves Shan had branded. The second impression he'd gotten had been when young O'Brien had mentioned seeing Sarahlee and Mary go past in the buggy. It wasn't as easy to define as the other impression, hadn't actually been anything more tangible than the look that had touched briefly on the cowboy's face.

He got down at the barn, off-saddled, and put up the horse. Maybe Ash had seen Mary up close; no one could deny she was pretty. He went to the cabin, poked up a fire in the stove, and put on the coffee pot. While waiting for it to boil, he drank a cup of whiskey. It made sweat burst out all over him. He stoked up his pipe and lit it, sat at the table with the door open, watching the sunlight dance over the barn like old brass.

When Sarahlee and Mary got back, they had two

sacks of flour and one of sugar in the back of the buggy. He carried them inside, put them down, and straightened up. Sarahlee was watching him.

"The doctor said it's true, Shan," she said, and when he raised his arms, she moved swiftly sideways toward the curtained-off bed. "It's sticky hot out. I'm going down to take a bath. You and Mary put the things away."

He watched her emerge from behind the curtain, go outside, down across the yard toward the spring house until she was cut off from sight.

"Shan?"

He turned, feeling a thousand years old, a thousand pounds heavy. Mary went up close, put her hands on his chest, and pressed them against him. He stared down at her for a moment, then caught her savagely and kissed her, ground his mouth over hers and felt the shattered burst of breath that was driven out of her. Then he pushed her away and started for the door.

"I'm going down by the dead fall tree this afternoon."

The dead fall was a toppled pine that had been shriven by lightning generations gone. Its trunk was barkless, gray, and smooth to the touch. Around the dead fall was a patch of soft, fine grass that was still green from a tiny seepage spring hidden in the tangle of rotten old wood.

He usually tied his horse in a gully that gaped fifty feet from the tree, but today he didn't. The animal dragged its reins through the underbrush, seeking green shoots. Shan was sitting there with his hat far back, sprawled and listless, when Mary rode up.

"I can't stay long, Shan."

"I know," he said roughly. "Get down. Come here."

Mary left her horse and it nosed over near Shan's. She went over beside Shan and sank down in the coolness and shade. Her face was very grave. She did not look at him and her hands lay together in her lap. "This is no good, Shan," she said, very low.

"Don't you think I know that," he said bitterly. "It's like water . . . when you start drinking, you can't stop." He put a heavy arm across her shoulders but made no other move. "I got a wife and I've got you."

"Trouble come someday, Shan. Trouble come and you be real mad at me."

He took his arm down, put his hand in her lap. She looked down at the thick fist, put a hand over it softly and closed her fingers. The contrast of rich golden color against his gray, rough skin was very noticeable. "Come over closer, Mary."

She did not move until he pulled at her. She kept her eyes away from his face.

"Are you worried, Mary?"

"Not worried, sad. She going to have a baby. No good, Shan."

"The baby'll get whatever it needs. So'll she and so'll you. There's nothing to worry about." He didn't believe it, but he wanted to. He'd take care of his child, sure; he'd also take care of Sarahlee and Mary.

"There isn't?" she asked, looking into his eyes for the first time. "You know there isn't anything to worry about, Shan?"

"Sure I know," he said, and kissed her.

For a while she looked at him very gravely, then she put her face against his chest and melted against him. Finally she looked up again and said: "It is like drinking watern. Get more, you want more. Too good, Shan, a big love too good. I love you. I told you that before. I don't know what more to say. I love you."

He drew her closer.

Over where the horses were there was movement. First one animal lifted its head, then the other one did. They stood like that, ears up, noses twitching, looking southward at a moving shadow. Shan and Mary did not notice them. Later the horses returned to grazing but every once in a while they would throw up their heads and stare far out.

CHAPTER SIXTEEN

An unexpected run of late summer calves just before haying time kept Shan busy for seven days, but when it was over, tired as he was, he felt good. He had not lost a calf that he knew of, nor a cow. For the most part there were no complications and that relieved him. Wherever he rode over his land, there were pairs, cows and calves. Some of the earlier calves were large now, shifting for themselves and gaining steadily. It required one full day to tally. Counting his split with Otto, there were over a hundred and sixty pairs. He rode with a deep-down smile that barely showed on his face. By next year at the same time he'd have some large animals to trail down and sell. In five years he'd have as many cattle as Otto had. He pocketed the tally sheet and sat his saddle with the contentment like wealth in his soul. He'd build onto the cabin, buy a brand new saddle, and maybe one of the short-running horses he'd heard the liveryman in Tico talking about.

There'd be money. They'd go visit Sarahlee's family, and he'd cut a swathe in Nebraska. When the shadows lengthened, he went home with a singing spirit. At the barn his smile drew down a little. For much of it he could thank the Blessings.

The next morning Otto showed up with his

team and wagon. It was time to start haying. Shan laughed aloud and said he'd hay the full length of Wyoming if Otto wanted to. Otto shook his head. Just the two ranches would be enough, he replied, and they went to work. The days spun out, grew shorter, and occasionally there would be a quick rush of cold wind down from the slopes with a scent and taste of snow fields to it. At night Shan would lie there, picturing sparkling new Red River wagons and brass-studded harness and new black hats and frilly dresses for Sarahlee, some close-fitting things for Mary. He'd build a separate cabin for Mary after the baby came; it would be better if she lived apart a little. Maybe he'd build it closer to the barn.

He and Otto hauled hay with two wagons and both teams until Shan's barn was full. Then they made fifty-ton stacks out on the range and built split-rail fences around them to keep the cattle from tearing them down, trampling them, after snow flew. It was grueling labor. Shan fell asleep at the late supper table almost every night. He drank prodigious amounts of water during the day and sweated it out.

Then they moved down to Otto's to hay, and Sarahlee and Mary came, too. The Mullers' house was like Christmas with women cooking and washing things and talking all the time while he and Otto worked the hay land, talked a little from time to time when they took a breather, and

200

planned ahead. Otto seemed a little more quiet, more thoughtful, every now and then, as though some strange mood was on him. Shan noticed but paid no heed.

The summer was almost over. It was just as hot during the days but around dawn the air would be sharp, have a winter smell and look to it. Autumn was closing down. There were several frosty nights.

Shan pitched hay onto the wagon and rode with its fragrance to the barn and pitched it over into the hay area and up into the loft until he could pitch hay in his sleep. He was like iron, glowing with health that showed in him like the glow of new money. It was a good way to be and he reveled in it. There was little to mar it, but there was something. Sarahlee wouldn't let him touch her, and she'd sit outside in the dusk with all of them after supper, sewing and humming to herself. She rarely joined the conversations any more. And Mary seemed to be avoiding him for some reason. Little things of no vast importance but he was conscious of them. One day Mary left before breakfast and didn't return until just before chore time. No one said anything about it, but one day, just before they finished haying Otto's place, Mary disappeared again, and that time Otto remarked on it.

"What the devil do you suppose she's up to, Shan? Could there be a buck around here some place she's seeing?"

"Now, Otto, she just needs the exercise is all.

You told me yourself they're different from us."

"Maybe," Otto conceded, "but I wish she'd say something ahead of time. That way I could single out a horse for her instead of her taking my old bay the way she does."

Then they all went up to Shan's to work cattle. The women went ahead in Otto's wagon. Sarahlee and Mrs. Muller gave the cabin a thorough cleaning. Otto and Shan, toned down from hard labor, ran in bunches of cattle and cut the bull calves, branded those Shan had missed, and made a notched-stick tally. They worked hard, ate heavy, and slept like dead men. One evening Shan brought a jug up from the spring house and they all sat around outside, watching the twilight. That was almost the last warm night of the year and it became something to be cherished, later. Something four of them at least never forgot.

When they were almost finished, Ash O'Brien and his older brother rode over from their own round-up camp. Shan had never met the older brother before. He looked like Ash, only larger, heavier, and his name was Tim. They hadn't been there an hour, drinking laced coffee and exchanging cow talk with Otto and Shan before their father, Will O'Brien, rode into the yard, dismounted, and tied his horse. From time to time the older man would raise his head and study Shan silently. So did Tim O'Brien. Young Ash was as friendly as ever. Sarahlee and Mrs. Muller had a jug of Indian cookies Mary had taught them to make. They served them with the coffee, and the men lounged in their chairs, eating and talking. Will O'Brien finally asked if either Shan or Otto had an iron thole pin. They had broken the one they used on their cook wagon and had no replacement. Otto said he didn't have one, but Shan told the O'Briens he had one and would be glad to sell it to him. Old Man O'Brien accepted the offer and gave Shan money to pay for the pin, then he took his boys and departed.

The next morning Shan left for town with Sarahlee's list and the list Otto gave him at the barn when he was harnessing the wagon team. Otto asked what time he thought he'd be back.

"As soon as I get the things loaded. No reason to hang around down there."

"Good," Otto said. "Fine." He sounded unnaturally relieved, and Shan looked down at him in a puzzled way from the wagon seat. Otto gave the near horse a pat on the rump and flagged with his hand. "We'll hang around here so's Sarahlee won't be alone until you get back." Then he turned without another look at Shan and started toward the cabin.

Shan looked after him with a vertical crease between his eyes. It was a strange way for Otto to act. He lifted the lines and his shoulders at the same time, dropped both, and hunched forward on the seat.

By the time he got to Tico, it was dinnertime. The sun was straight overhead. He went to the Mercantile and crossed off the things he wanted as he and an elderly clerk grunted with them to the wagon. By the time he was loaded, it was late afternoon. At the smithy he had to wait while the blacksmith beat out several thole pins and sold three of them to Shan. By then it was almost sundown, too late to start the trek back. He drove the laden wagon to the livery barn, left it parked securely out back where its contents couldn't be stolen, paid for a pair of tie stalls, some hay and grain for the team, crossed the dusty roadway to a café, and studied the list as he ate. He had everything he'd been sent for. He leaned back with a good feeling, lit his pipe, and smoked. The world looked good. Later, he went to the saloon and polished off three cups of Green River, then went back outside, feeling more expansive and comfortable than ever. They'd be expecting him home in another hour or two, but when he didn't show up by 9:00 or so they'd figure he'd decided to stay over.

He was standing in the waning light when a group of range men went flashing past, spurs and rein chains ringing. One reckless face turned, saw him, and broke into a wide, toothy grin. The group was fifteen feet farther down the thoroughfare when the grinning face called out: "Howdy, Squawman! Hey, fellers, there's Otto Muller's Abe Lincoln boy yonder. . . ."

They swirled down the shadowy lane with only the echo of their jingle and creak lingering where Shan stood. He drew up slowly and twisted to see where they halted, but traffic and the dusk kept them from him. He turned and began to walk southward on the plank walk. He wasn't angry exactly, just ready to see some excitement. Willing to take issue over that name.

But he didn't find them. He visited four saloons but didn't see anyone who grinned like that or said anything to him. He saw a lot of riders and they saw him, but not a one of them spoke. Then he met Tim O'Brien on the plank walk and invited him in for a drink. O'Brien turned him down, said he rarely ever drank, and Shan replied that Tim was the first Irishman he'd ever run across who wouldn't drink the spots off a bar top. O'Brien looked straight at him without replying.

"You drank laced coffee up at my place yesterday," Shan said.

"Yes, that was a sociable drink. I don't drink much ever, Mister Shanley, and never at all in town."

"It won't hurt you," Shan insisted. "You know, O'Brien, when I was in the Army you'd get judged by how much whiskey you could hold."

"I don't judge folks," Tim O'Brien said with a growing edge to his tone, "and I don't like them judging me."

"Who's judging you?" Shan said in surprise,

then he looked at O'Brien a moment before turning away. "Fellers like you make me sick," he said.

"Shanley! Oh, forget it . . . you're drunk."

Shan turned back slowly. "Who's drunk? Why you damned fool, I've drunk more whiskey than you have water, and I can count the times I've been drunk on the fingers of one hand."

"Then you'd better start using the fingers on the other hand right now," O'Brien said. "I know when a man's drunk." There was a hard light in his eyes.

Shan walked back a few steps and for a moment he said nothing. They were nearly of a size but Shan, even trimmed down and stone hard, was easily twenty pounds heavier. He dropped his gaze to O'Brien's high-heeled boots and smiled. "You wouldn't know a drunk if one hit you," he said, "teetering around on those silly boots like a dance-hall girl."

O'Brien's eyes were very still, his face grew pale, and when he spoke, his voice was even softer than before. "Maybe I think the same about fellers who wear those flat-heeled squatter's boots," he said.

"Squatter's boots?" Shan looked down. "Drover's boots you mean."

"No, I mean squatter's boots. Squatters . . . fellers who come along and take up rangeland others been running cattle on for ten years . . . squatters."

Shan raised his head. Excitement moved in the depths of his eyes; he was almost grinning. "If I'm a squatter, why I expect I'm the first one that ever turned O'Brien cattle back off my range then."

"Listen, Shanley . . ." The words were soft but razor-edged. A few bystanders were drawing close, winking to one another.

"Listen yourself, you dance-hall heifer."

"I wish it'd been me instead of my brother you talked so hard to that day you met our herd going out."

Shan's ire was beginning to rise a little. "Talked hard to? That's a damned lie. I just told him I needed my feed is all, and if that's talking hard, O'Brien, I expect you'd better get used . . ."

O'Brien's fist streaked outward without any warning. Shan didn't see it coming until it exploded under his jaw, and he went over backward. He wasn't hurt, just bowled off balance. Looking up, he saw the bystanders, grown to a considerable crowd now, grinning wider than ever as he got to his knees. Men were calling to their friends. Shan was back on his feet before he understood what they were saying.

"Come on. That squawman and Tim O'Brien're mixing it."

He hurtled himself at O'Brien. "Squawman! Who're you calling a squawman!"

O'Brien was as fast as a cat but he was no match for big Ryan Shanley, not even when Shan wasn't fighting mad. "Whose a squawman!" Shan bellowed at the top of his lungs. "I'll show you who's a squawman . . . an Abe Lincoln boy . . . !"

After the first brief exchange of blows, Shan struck O'Brien almost at will. Nothing O'Brien had hit him with could check his forward momentum. The difference between them was essentially that Tim O'Brien couldn't hit hard and Shan could. He'd been hitting since his orphanage days. In the Army he'd learned how and when and where to hit. He had scars acquired from twenty years of fighting, and now, slightly over thirty, he was a rugged and experienced fighter, which Tim O'Brien was not.

A tearing blow that caught O'Brien under the ear, after a thunderous slam had half turned him, ended the fight. Shan stood, wide-legged, looking at the unconscious form, half on, half off the plank walk, in the purple dust of the darkened roadway.

"Who else's got those squawman notions?" he challenged the crowd, stone-still and silent now, sobered. "Who else wants to get a little piece of an Abe Lincoln boy? Come on . . . !" He swore at them, but no one came forward and a few on the outskirts drifted away. The others watched him with all the respect they'd show a crouched cougar, lashing its tail.

He turned and shouldered roughly past them, was almost clear of the faces when behind him a man in the crowd with the guns and spurs of a rider lifted a hand high and brought it down hard. There was a sullen shine of blue steel seconds before the crunch of metal over bone, and Shan collapsed without a sound.

When he came around later, his head ached fiercely. He got up out of the dirt and saw that Tim O'Brien was gone, and there was a hush around him. He crossed to a watering trough and washed his head, probed the bump, guessed with no effort how he had acquired it, and went down to the livery barn. The night swamper nodded to him in total silence and busied himself with a hand-barrow and a shovel. He climbed to the loft, buried himself in the hay, and tried to sleep and forget. A little scimitar-shaped moon shone through gaping mow doors.

He was hitching up an hour before dawn. By daybreak he was well up the stage road, north-ward. There wasn't a rider anywhere in sight. He surmised the O'Brien outfit must have pulled out of Tico the night before, probably not long after they'd patched up their boss' son. At the Muller place he pulled in and watered the team, made a cigarette, and looked solemnly at the empty house, smoked, and felt like swearing at himself. What resentment still lingered was directed at the coward who had struck him over the head from behind.

Squawman! It hadn't been just that blurry rider, loping past. Those men in the crowd had called him that as well. He thought of young Ash O'Brien, the way he'd looked at Mary the time she had been with Shan and they'd met. And later, how he spoke of seeing Sarahlee and Mary—"The Injun girl."—he'd said. Dull anger stirred and grew and simmered. That was where it had started.

He drove out of Otto's yard and angled toward the road. Later, when he got home, he set the brake in front of the cabin and got down. Otto and Mrs. Muller crowded up along with Sarahlee. They all helped carry what belonged to the Shanleys inside. Otto's things were left in the wagon, and Shan walked beside the team to the barn, where he was unharnessing when Otto appeared in the doorway, eyes watching Shan, his little pipe going.

"Anything new in town?"

"I got into a fight, Otto."

Otto's eyes widened a trifle. "Who with?"

"Tim O'Brien."

"Tim?" Otto said in surprise. "Why, Tim's no fighter, Shan. I mean, he don't start fights. I've known him for eight years and have yet to see him give offence."

"I guess it was my fault," Shan said. "We were joshing and one thing led to another, and he busted me one. When I got up, I knocked him out."

Otto looked unbelieving. "Well," he said finally,

"dog-gone it. You know those O'Briens are about the squarest folks around here, Shan."

Shan straightened up, passed Otto to throw the harness into the wagon box. "It was a damned fool thing," he said.

"Did you have a few drinks before it happened?"

Shan felt irritated but he nodded his head meekly enough. "I expect that's what it was . . . but I'd eaten."

Otto knocked out his pipe and squinted at the sun. "Well, let's get some dinner."

"Here," Shan said, holding out a thole pin. "I got three of them. One for you, and two for me."

Otto stuck the pin into his trouser pocket and crossed the yard beside Shan. After they had eaten, they both went down to the spring house and took a bath. The water made Shan feel a lot better. He began to search his mind for justification for the fight and found plenty but it wasn't anything he could tell Otto so he didn't speak of it again.

The Mullers drove home that evening. The next day and the day after Shan spent splitting logs and snaking them down to the yard to weather. He meant to use them the next spring for building the fence around the hay fields. The third day Otto rode up with a shotgun across his lap.

"Been sage hen hunting. Figured you might like to come along."

Shan was grateful for the diversion, and although he had only a few loads for his scatter-gun, he saddled up, tied his sheepskin coat aft of the cantle, and told Sarahlee where he was going.

They rode west of the barn, out through the hayed-off land, but didn't stir up a single sage chicken. Otto struck out across the road then.

"Probably be better over here," he said.

By the time they came upon the abandoned range camp of the O'Brien outfit, they had seen several of the ungainly birds and had bagged two. "Too bad you had that fight, Shan. The O'Briens are your nearest neighbors next to us, son."

"I'm sorry, too," Shan said, poking at the rubble left behind at the cow camp. "I'll apologize next time I run across O'Brien."

"If he lets you," Otto said, grunting back into the saddle. "I expect there were a lot of fellows standing around when you whipped him, weren't there?"

"There was quite a bunch before it was over."

"Yeah," Otto said. "Well now, folks in Wyoming are a little different than other folks that way, Shan. You can apologize to Tim, and he might even accept it, but I know his paw. Old Will won't be so quick to forgive and forget. He'll expect you to apologize in town, Shan. Maybe some Saturday when there'll be the same crowd handy to hear you."

Shan looked disbelievingly at Otto and his face darkened. "I'll be . . ."

"Now wait a minute," Otto interrupted. "Maybe you were right in whipping Tim for all I know. I'm just telling you how folks out here look at those things. You've got to eat the same humble pie you made Tim eat when you licked him in front of a crowd."

"I couldn't do that, Otto."

"I don't expect it was pleasant for Tim, either, boy."

"He asked for it."

Otto's eyes flashed for a moment, then he said: "I'm saying the O'Briens are good neighbors, Shan. If you're going to keep them that way, you've got to make up for hitting Tim."

They rode on for a half mile more before Shan drew up when a sage chicken whirred out of the broken grass in front of them, and Otto dismounted, ran forward a little, and fired at it. He missed and swore.

"I guess I've got to do it, Otto. I guess they'll be a little mad at you, too."

"I can stand that," Otto said, remounting. "I'm thinking of all of us living and working out here, Shan. There's no sense in having to turn away when you see a man riding past. Especially over something as silly as a fistfight between you and Tim. You'll help them and they'll help you as the years go by."

"All right."

Shan felt better as soon as he said it. They rode until the shadows caught them, then turned back for Shan's place. They had six prairie chickens. Otto had gotten four, Shan two.

They parted at the road, and Shan crossed the yard in a stiff trot, put up the horse, fed, milked the little brindle cow, and went to the cabin. It was cheerful with orange lamplight. He gave the feathery trophies to Mary and sat down at the table and sighed.

"Is it cold out?" Sarahlee asked.

"It's getting cold," he replied. "I sort of hate to see fall come. It's like something is going away that will never come back again."

Later he went to bed and Sarahlee cradled his head on her arm. They didn't speak to one another, and he eventually fell asleep.

CHAPTER SEVENTEEN

During those autumnal days Shan noticed how quickly the shadows fell, how much earlier day ended. Then there were the brittle fleckings of frost, at first only in the morning, but later in the evenings, too. Mary would put some stove-length wood into the firebox just before they all retired to keep the cold away an hour or so longer.

Sarahlee had sent for some books and Shan read them. One was the Bible. It was difficult for him to comprehend, but he enjoyed *Pilgrim's Progress*. Her family sent copies of old newspapers that he studied with interest. Then one bright, cold day with the sun high, but without warmth, Otto rode up and said he had quite a few late calves down at his place that the O'Briens had found and driven over, and they needed to be cut before it got too cold. Shan welcomed the diversion for he had been becoming restless. Sarahlee and Mary were getting on his nerves. The everlasting stillness, the sameness of existence without work, were beginning to pall on him.

They rode down to Otto's, worked the cattle, ate heaps of hot food, and drank a little whiskey, then Otto brought out a leather ledger book and began squaring his account of the cattle with Shan. Later, when everything else had been taken care of, he told Shan he intended to drive a herd of two-year-old steers and cull cows to Tico.

"How come to Tico? I thought you said you had to drive to the railhead to sell."

"You usually do, but I happened onto a buyer at Tico a few days back and he said he'd take delivery there because he's trying to make up a trail herd for Kansas from this district."

"Oh. Well, I've seen the corrals south of town. Maybe next year I'll help you fill them."

Otto closed the ledger and smiled. "You ought to be able to," he said. "You've got a big start in the cattle business this year."

They corral-cut the cattle and drove the animals to be sold five miles down the road in order to get a head start the following dawn. They couldn't make any time at all without having the cattle take a weight loss and yet Otto wanted to make Tico before nightfall.

The next dawn they were on horseback with their breaths showing white and filmy in the crackling cold, picked up the cattle, and began the drive southward. They were dressed warmly and Otto had a flask with him. The cattle followed the road docilely and after several hours the drive became monotonous. They made good time but did not corral the animals until the sun was down. While they were putting up their horses, Shan eyed the lighted saloons with interest. They went across the road to a small café and filled up on hot food. The place was unclean, had steamed windows and greasy air, but the cold drive had given them both prodigious appetites. To top off the meal Shan offered to buy Otto a drink, and they went down the plank walk to the closest saloon, which did not have many people in it. Otto had a jolt of Green River. They stood around for a while, then Otto said he was tired. They went to the hotel, got a room, and bedded down.

At dawn they were astir. Otto crossed to the livery barn and bought a wagonload of hay that he and Shan pitched to the corralled cattle, then they went back to the same café and had breakfast.

Time hung heavily after that. Otto left word at the hotel for the cattle buyer, then he and Shan went down by the corrals and sat in the sunlight, whittling and talking.

About noon another drive came in. Shan knew none of the men but Otto did. The owner and trail boss was James Monroe, who studied Shan's face and size when Otto introduced them but said very little. When his animals were cared for, Monroe took his three riders uptown for a drink.

Right after the Monroe riders left, a short, bull-like man in a plug hat drove up in mud-splattered cut-under runabout with a beautiful black gelding between the shafts. He nodded briskly to Shan and began joking with Otto. He was the cattle buyer and Shan noticed that he chewed tobacco constantly and had sharp, very light-colored gray eyes. While the buyer and Otto crawled over the corral and walked among the cattle, talking, Shan lounged in the sun, watching traffic ebb and flow. It seemed that Tico had more people stirring than usual. He thought little of that until the buyer and Otto returned and were leaning on the corral while the buyer wrote out the Kansas City bank draft for the cattle. When the buyer said the date, Shan understood it was Saturday. Ranch people holidayed in town on Saturday.

The cattle were bawling, stirring up dust. Shan bent, picked up a pebble, and tossed it up and down on his palm. James Monroe and his riders walked past, trading silent nods with him and heading for the buyer. Shan thought the glance of Monroe was too appraising, the looks of his riders too lingering. He threw the stone away.

Otto came over folding the draft carefully. He wore a satisfied look. "Well," he said, "that makes the seventh drive I've made and the second I've sold in Tico. Let's go pay off what I owe at the Mercantile. I'll leave the draft there. They'll get it cashed for me and keep the balance in their safe until I'm down here again."

Shan could look head and shoulders over most of the people they passed *en route*. At the store the low hum of voices droned ceaselessly. Otto left the draft, signed a slip authorizing the merchant to withhold from his funds what he owed, got a receipt, and lead Shan across the road to a saloon. There they had two drinks and Otto bought a jug, then they went to the livery barn and got their horses. The liveryman gave Shan a broad, raffish smile when he handed him the reins. Shan thought it was an unnecessarily familiar smile.

They rode through the pleasant afternoon, sucking on Otto's jug and talking of different things. Otto grew mellow and talkative.

"This winter Georgia'll be driving up whenever the snow's not too deep. She's an awful good hand at most things. We never had any kids but she'll know exactly what to do. And you could maybe build onto the cabin, make a porch all around to give plenty of summer shade and a dry place to pile winter wood."

"I figure to do those things," Shan said, "and chop a lot more wood."

"Yes, after a while you'll get so's you'll know just which way a tree's going to fall and just how to bust a chunk of stove-length wood so's it'll break into four pieces." Otto grinned. "By summertime I usually get to looking at that damned woodbox like it was a personal enemy. I can fill it three times a day, but every time I pass it there's always room for another armload." He held out the jug. "You'll see what I mean before spring. It makes a feller understand how those men living by themselves in the high country get crazy after a while."

Shan watched the deepening color sweep in low and silky. He drank and returned the jug to Otto who looped a saddle thong through the handle and let the jug sway gently against his leg. Up ahead a cow bawled faintly; it was a lonely sound. Then other critters took it up and Otto stiffened in his saddle, straining to see.

"There's a drive coming," he said.

Shan squinted at the far distance where shadows were closing in. "They won't get near Tico tonight," he said.

"They're probably already bedded down. You can't drive after sunset or you lose half your herd."

By the time they were close enough to smell

the supper fire, there were dark, moving objects around them, the pungent scent of cattle, and sounds of their clicking horns. A bright fire burned east of the road a ways and Shan followed Otto toward it. He recognized the riders as they unwound off the ground and stood in silence, peering up at them—the O'Briens.

Otto got down, went up to the fire, and beat his cold hands together. He greeted each O'Brien and their riders by first names, and back where Shan stood, holding their horses, the answers sounded thinly courteous and reserved. He dropped the reins and walked in closer. Ash O'Brien turned and saw him.

"Good evening," Shan said.

Ash nodded without smiling and looked away. Tim O'Brien was standing across the fire from him. Old Will was to one side of his older son, staring at Shan with a stony expression.

Otto bent over the fire. "Why didn't you corral at my place?" he said genially. "No sense in staying out here in the cold."

"No need to," Will O'Brien said shortly.

"No," Otto agreed, "No need, but you usually do, Will. Shan and I're just getting back. I sold down in Tico this morning. That slaughterhouse buyer out of Kansas is down there, making up a trail herd. Jim Monroe got in about noon or a little before." He was looking at the steaming coffee pot as he spoke.

Will O'Brien took his antagonistic glance off Shan and made a gesture to Otto. "Help yourself," he said.

While Otto poured coffee, Shan knew he was waiting for him to say what must be said. He took in a big breath of cold night air. "Tim?"

"Yes."

"I had no call to do what I did in Tico. I wish you'd accept my apology." It cost something to say it and Shan was grateful for the darkness because the three O'Briens, their three riders, and Otto were all standing perfectly still, looking at him. "I had no right to start that fight . . . I want to apologize for doing it."

Tim stood across the fire, peering at Shan from beneath the sweep of his hat brim, face mottled by flickering firelight. At first he said nothing.

Ash squatted down and poked at the fire, threw on some twigs from a little pile beside him. Will O'Brien accepted the cup of hot coffee Otto held out toward him without taking his eyes off Shan. "You got a lot to learn," he said. "The first thing is that picking fights is apt to leave your wife a widow. The second thing is that no matter how big you are . . . out here that don't count for much unless you're powerful good with a gun, too." The old man was silent a moment, then he shrugged and looked down at the fire. "It's up to Tim," he said, "but I'm going to tell you one more thing, Shanley. The next time you start a fight, you're going to get killed."

Shan swallowed, found his throat burning-dry. Anger was building up in him. He took the tongue-lashing because he knew what Otto was thinking, standing there, holding his cup and watching him. Then Tim O'Brien spoke.

"I reckon it wasn't all your fault, Shanley. We just didn't hit it off that night." He moved closer to the little fire and held his hand out. Shan gripped it, pumped it once, and drew his hand back. From off to one side and below them young Ash held something up toward Shan.

"Cup of coffee?"

The old man and Otto walked down by the saddled horses, talking. When they came into the wavering firelight, Otto had the jug. The old man would listen when Shan spoke but did not look at him. Of the O'Brien crew he alone remained reserved right up to the time Shan and Otto left the camp. Ash was the friendliest, the riders seemed willing to forget, and even Tim O'Brien smiled when Shan and Otto wheeled and rode out into the night.

When they were riding up the road again, Shan said: "That stiff-necked old devil."

Otto was frowningly searching for the turn-off into his place from the road when he replied. "He's had a hard pull out here, Shan. He's been here longer'n any of us, and when he started out, you had to fight Indians every morning before you rode out to hunt cattle. But I'll tell you this. Will O'Brien's one of the best neighbors you'll ever have . . . don't you forget it."

"I apologized."

"I know, but if he could make you feel lower'n a snake's belly . . . rub salt in you so's you'd really feel ashamed . . . he'd do it. If you didn't get mad . . . and you didn't . . . why old Will would accept the apology and call it a closed affair so far as he's concerned. That's his nature. But there's one thing he said you don't ever want to forget . . . that part about getting killed for starting fights. He meant it. That's the way folks live out here." Otto reined into the cut-off and let his horse pick his own way toward the dark barn beyond. "You ought to know that after what happened with the Blessings."

Shan left Otto and rode on home. It was after midnight when he put up his horse and crossed the frozen yard to the cabin. Just before he reached the door, a shadow detached itself from the corner of the house. He saw it from the corner of his eye and spun, the pistol leaping into his cold fingers, swinging to aim.

"Shan?"

"Mary!" He straightened up and quick anger seized him. He lowered the pistol. "What do you mean slipping up on me like that? Are you crazy? I might have shot you."

She moved up close, groped for his free hand,

and tugged at him. He resisted. "Please, Shan. . . ." He let her lead him back across the yard to the barn. When they were in the pale glow of a frozen moon, she swung to face him, dropped his hand.

"Shan? I missed you."

"What's the matter with you, Mary?" he said sullenly, scowling down into her face. "What if Sarahlee came awake while we were out here? You just aren't using your head at all any more, it seems like."

"I don't want you to be mean to me, Shan." There was a tremor in her voice he'd never heard there before.

He continued to scowl at her. She loved him, loved him until it hurt. Well, he'd never intended for her to get it *that* bad. While he was standing there, watching her, an echo of a derisive cry came back to him. *Squawman*. His eyes kindled with cold fire. Like hell he was! Squawmen lived with them. Lived in a hide tent and wore Indian tanned-skin pants and shirts and had coffee-colored kids.

"Shan . . . hold me?"

He held her, felt the deep roll of her heart through his shirt, and smelled the scent in her hair and couldn't raise any interest in her at all. After a moment he pushed her back and said: "We'd better get inside. I'll go first, and I'll leave the door open and you listen . . . when I'm making noise behind the curtain, you slip in and be damned quiet. Go to bed, understand?"

"I understand. But, Shan, I want to see you. I want to talk with you. Please . . . ?"

He left her at the barn, crossed the hard ground, and opened the cabin door, removed his boots, and left them near the opening, tossed his hat on the table, and removed his heavy coat. He stalked toward the partition, listening for Sarahlee's breathing. He could dimly make her out. Chestnut hair splayed out around her face, she was hard asleep. He undressed and climbed into the bed. When it made a protesting groan, he thought he also heard a swish of movement, the gentle whisper of a door closing. He gritted his teeth and worked his way under the pile of quilts.

He slept until nearly 9:00 a.m. the following morning, and when he awakened, he was alone in the bed. Beyond the curtain he heard movement.

"Sarahlee, is that you?"

Instead of answering, she came around the partition and smiled down at him. "You must have gotten back pretty late. Go ahead and rest if you want to."

"No," he said, and got up.

"I've kept breakfast warm."

He went outside and washed. The sun was up, but there was a steely veil across it and the frost hadn't left the ground. The tang of wood smoke hung in the motionless air, rose straight up like a thin, dirty rope from the stovepipe. He breathed in a lot of the wintery scent and dried himself on the bitterly cold towel that had his initials darned across it. The corralled horses nickered at him. Everywhere he looked, things stood out, sharp and crystal-clear. The fat old mountains seemed miles closer, their tiers of trees aged with hoarfrost high up. The big barn crackled where the sun struck it and the spring house glistened.

He went inside, put on his shirt, and ate while Sarahlee asked about the drive. He drank a second cup of coffee while he told her, then he went back out and fed the livestock. When he was finishing up, he saw that one horse was missing. He went where the saddle usually hung and found it also gone. Mary!

He went on doing chores like milking and dunging out, hanging around down at the barn, wondering what to do next until restlessness made him cross the yard, seeking tracks. When he found them, they pointed east. He took the milk to the cabin and hung around there for a while before he spoke.

"Where did Mary go, Sarahlee?"

"I don't know. She wasn't here when I got up. I thought she'd gone down to feed for you like she does sometimes."

"She's gone riding," he said.

Sarahlee looked up from straining the milk. "Cold out for pleasure riding, isn't it?"

"Yes," he said, "but the horse she took is that one I used for the drive. He needs a few days' rest."

"Well, don't say anything to her when she comes back, Shan. One of these days she'll understand those things. Just be patient with her like I try to be."

Sarahlee began humming as she worked. It grated on his nerves, so he went back outside. For two hours he worked at marking off the porch he meant to build that winter and by the end of that time he knew Mary wasn't going to return until late and his anger increased. When Sarahlee called him in to eat, he sat down heavily and said: "Damned squaw."

"Shan!"

"Well, why didn't she take one of the other horses?"

"Don't get upset over it, Shan. The horse will survive and you'll feel ashamed later, if you say anything to her. You get upset too easily, dear."

"Right now I got a reason to be," he said. "That horse's had all the use he can stand since we started working the cattle. He needs a rest. Why couldn't she take one of the others, anyway? She doesn't use her head sometimes, Sarahlee."

"She's young, Shan, and this summer hasn't been easy for her."

"It hasn't been easy for any of us. Work, work, work!"

Sarahlee dried her hands and went over behind his chair, leaned down, and put her arms around his neck, brushed her cheek across his hair, and held him without speaking. It worked like it always did. He relaxed against her, and most of the winteriness left his eyes.

She stood up and took her arms away, ran fingers through his hair, then went back to the stove. "It isn't as important as you're making out," she said. "It was thoughtless, inconsiderate perhaps, but she's only a child, you know. I think she deserves better from us because she's acquired a vocabulary of several hundred words and doesn't have hardly any accent left at all, has learned to cook and sew. She's really very remarkable, Shan. Georgia says she's the most intelligent Indian she's ever seen. Georgia's very fond of Mary."

Shan stood up suddenly. "By golly, Sarahlee," he said, "I'll bet you that's where she went . . . down to the Muller place."

"It probably is," Sarahlee agreed. "Shan, Mary's an individual, too. She's got to have friends, go visit them just like we do." Sarahlee sighed softly. "Maybe one of these days a handsome young civilized Indian boy will come along for her."

Shan went back outside where his tools lay. He stood a moment, scanning the countryside before he returned to work. There was no sign of Mary.

CHAPTER EIGHTEEN

Mary returned late in the evening. Shan was washing up outside and heard her ride in. He looked around toward the barn angrily, but Sarahlee was standing in the doorway, talking to him. He put his head down and kept his mouth closed. He didn't even speak to Mary at supper. Later, when she and Sarahlee were doing the dishes and he was smoking his pipe outside, looking over the measurements of the proposed porch, he heard them talking. Sarahlee was being motherly and remonstrative in her gentle way. It made him want to laugh.

The next morning, after he'd done the chores and eaten, he was outside, checking the level lines he'd put up the day before, when Sarahlee came to the doorway with a worried look.

"Shan, Otto wants to see you. He told Mary to ask you to ride down."

He looked around at her. "What does he want?"

"I have no idea. He didn't tell Mary. Do you suppose Georgia is ill?"

"I guess I'd better saddle up and ride down."

He was turning away when Sarahlee said: "Do you suppose I ought to go with you?"

He considered it, decided it wasn't necessary. "Probably a sick cow or something like that," he said.

Sarahlee appeared undecided. She was large and pink in the doorway. He unconsciously looked at her middle; she was swelling noticeably now. Then he said: "I suppose if it had been anything serious, he'd have told Mary." She disappeared into the cabin.

He rode through the crisp morning with pale sunlight lighting his way. When he got to the barn, Otto was out back with a blanket coat on, cleaning feeders. He had his unlit pipe between his teeth, and when Shan rode up, swung down, and greeted him, Otto beckoned him into the barn.

Otto had a jug out there. The first thing he did was hold it out.

Shan took a pull and spat. "Something wrong, Otto?"

"Sit down, Shan."

Shan dropped down on the log mudsill, put the jug between them, and looked into the lined face. "Something wrong about the cattle?" he asked.

"No. I got something to tell you." Shan had never seen Otto agitated before. He knew from experience you couldn't rush Otto, so he relaxed and leaned back, looking out the doorway toward the house. There was a wispy spiral of smoke coming out of the chimney.

"I'd rather be shot than tell you this," Otto began. "I guess you'll get mad at me, too."

Shan looked around. He was puzzled but felt no particular foreboding. "I wouldn't get mad at you, Otto," he said. "Why, I owe you folks just about everything I have."

"I got no business butting into this, Shan. It's none of my damned business." Otto looked past Shan at the back of his house. "Mary came down here yesterday."

"I know, darn her copper hide. She took the same horse I used on the drive and never told either of us anything . . . just up and rode off like she does every once in a while."

"I know," Otto said. "She did that the time we were all down here, remember?"

"Yes, I remember."

"That time she went to Tico."

Shan looked surprised. "Tico? How do you know that? What would she go to Tico for?"

"Shan, Mary's pregnant."

"She's *what?*"

"Pregnant."

Shan leaped up with his big fists doubled. "That's a lie!" he shouted. The color was gone from his face.

Otto ignored it. "She's going to have a baby. That trip to Tico was to make sure. Yesterday she came to see Georgia. They've always been pretty close. . . ."

"Otto! Georgia'll tell Sarahlee!"

"No she won't."

Shan went across the aisle of the barn to a tie-stall partition and slumped against it.

"Shan, I got something else to tell you about this. I heard it a couple of times in town. Fellers riding after cattle saw you and Mary at different times. The whole countryside knows about it."

Hey, squawman. . . .

"Otto," Shan said in a near whisper, "what do I do now?"

"I don't know. But sooner or later Sarahlee's going to find out. If I were you, I think I'd be the first to tell her, Shan."

"That's crazy, Otto. I can't do that. I can't tell my wife I got a squaw pregnant."

"I don't know what else you can do," Otto said.

"I'll get rid of Mary."

Otto picked up the jug, took a long swallow from it, and set it down. He didn't say anything.

"I'll send her to that Indian school I heard about down in Colorado."

"I went to Tico last night," Otto said quietly, "and talked to the Indian agent down there. That school doesn't take pregnant girls, Shan."

"Why not? An Indian's an Indian, isn't it?"

"Here, take a drink."

"It'd make me heave . . . no thanks."

The minutes dragged by in silence. Otto was slumped against the wall in his blanket coat, looking at the jug.

"I've got to get rid of her, Otto. I've got to."

"Shan, don't do something that's going to haunt you the rest of your life."

"I didn't mean shoot her."

"I didn't think you meant that," Otto said sharply, in a tone Shan would have been surprised at any other time.

"I'll find out where her people are and send her back to them."

"They wouldn't take her back now, Shan. Indians look at this about like we do. They'd run her out of the tribe, maybe beat her in the bargain."

"All right," Shan said hotly, "you've been killing every idea I get . . . let's hear one good one from you."

"I don't know any. I only know what you *can't* do."

"But, Otto, I can't let her stay around. Sarahlee's bound to notice pretty soon."

"Tell Sarahlee."

"That's impossible, you know that," Shan said. Then: "Does Georgia know?"

"She's the one who told me. Mary told her. Mary's scairt sick. She doesn't know what to do and she knows your wife's going to see it one of these days. You know, Shan, I told you a long time ago what was happening inside that girl. Georgia could see it, too."

"I wish I'd gotten rid of her then," Shan said.

"Well, that's all done and past now."

"Your wife's going to hate me, Otto. That hurts worse than the other."

"No, Shan, she feels sorry for you. For all three of you."

"Why can't I just give Mary some money and a horse and send her off?"

Otto picked up the jug and swirled it absently, then set it down. "You'd never forget doing that, Shan. You'd think of it every night you couldn't sleep. You'd always wonder if she died in a snowbank somewhere. You'd feel pretty low for making her face it alone all the rest of your life. That's why you can't do that."

"Then what *can* I do?"

"I told you. I don't know, but I *do* know that this will get found out sooner or later, and I don't expect Sarahlee'd ever forgive you if you let her find it out for herself."

"And your wife . . . .?"

"Never mind her, she's older."

"What's age got to do with it?"

"Plenty. You'll know when you're my age."

Shan crossed the aisle, picked up the jug, tilted his head far back, and let the whiskey gush down his gullet, set the jug down, and began to fill his pipe. When he lit it, the taste was flat and bitter.

"I'm going home, Otto. I've got to think."

Otto got heavily to his feet. "I did my thinking last night and this morning," he said, and watched Shan go to his mount, give the cinch a little tug, toe in, and spring up, whirl the beast, and lope northward, then he started toward the house with the jug dangling from his hand. His wife was watching him from the doorway.

Shan rode with the feeling that every joint in him was made of putty, his backbone a length of rubber. When he was close enough to see his cabin and barn, he jerked the horse easterly and went on past.

His cattle, his ranch, his wife—what would happen to them now? The horse slowed at last, picked its own way down to the deadfall, and stopped. Shan sat there, staring at the dead-gray old trunk, hating it with all his soul.

He got down and threw up his arms and swore. It made the cold, brittle sunlight reverberate with sound. Then he stood stockstill and told himself he wasn't going to lose anything, wasn't going to be hurt. But the truth loomed larger than ever. Just a wife was all, just a big beautiful girl with his child in her was all. Just everything he'd worked harder to get than he'd ever worked in his life was all. Just everything: respect of neighbors, the dreams of how things were going to be, those soft, velvety evenings Otto had talked about, after the work was done. That was all he was going to lose. *Squawman!* It was all over the countryside already, not as Otto said it would be— not later. It didn't matter about Tico, about the O'Briens and the Monroe outfit that had looked at him strangely down at Tico's corrals. Those things made him know the depths of humiliation, of shame, but they weren't important. What *was* important was Sarahlee—and the Mullers—like folks to him, the Mullers.

He'd tell Sarahlee, like Otto said. He'd *have* to tell her. He didn't fear her wrath; it was the way he knew she would look at him. He shrank away from that in his thoughts.

The sun drifted down beyond the road some-where, still wearing its veil of steel, and shadows hastened from under things, spread out, low and thick, to join with the cold.

Tell her. That's all there was left to do. Tell her and die a hundred times while she listened and looked up into his face.

He mounted his horse, thinking of Mary, wishing she were a buck Indian. He'd ride into the yard and call out, and when the dark skin showed, the black obsidian eyes, he'd shoot her right there in the yard. He struck the saddle horn with a fist and told himself he was thinking crazy. If Mary'd been a buck Indian, it wouldn't have happened.

He rode westerly with the dying blood-red light on his face, saw his cabin and his barn, and for the first time he rode toward them without eager-ness. Sarahlee crossed the yard when she heard him ride up.

"What was it, Shan?"

He fumbled stiffly with the latigo. "What?"

"What did Otto want?"

"Oh . . . just talk." He kept his back to her as he

lifted the saddle, hung it by one stirrup on its peg, went back to remove the blanket and bridle.

She watched him with a faint frown. "Shan, it was more than just talk. I can see it in your face. What's wrong?"

He put the horse in a tie stall, forked him some hay, hung up the bridle in silence, and began to drape the sweaty blanket over the saddle.

"Shan!"

"I don't want to tell you, Sarahlee."

She went over and turned him to face her with one hand. She stood so close that the thrust of her bosom was hard against his shirt. It was like being struck with something, personal contact with her right then.

"You've *got* to tell me, Shan. I'm your wife. We share everything. Your troubles are mine, too. Now tell me!"

"This is going to kill everything, Sarahlee."

"What arc you talking about? What do you mean?" She was frightened now.

"Mary's going to have a baby."

"Mary? Is that what Otto told you?"

"Yes."

"How could he know? You mean *our* Mary?"

"Mary told Missus Muller."

"Yesterday, Shan? Is that where she went when she took your horse?"

"Yes."

"But it isn't possible, Shan."

"Yes it is."

She read the answer to her unspoken question in his face. She wavered backward just the smallest bit. "You?"

He nodded.

"You?"

He did not answer and a muscle twitched in his cheek. Sarahlee moved farther away, walked to the manger, and let herself down slowly. When he crossed to her, she turned her face away. He stopped ten feet from her and the silence roared in his head.

Ride away, he thought. *Saddle up and ride away, disappear. Head into the bloody sun and keep on riding forever.* After a while Sarahlee got up and left the barn. He did not follow her. *It's this ranch,* he told himself, *four men's ghosts haunt it . . . make things happen like this.* There was a little pool of water seeping from beneath the spring house floor. *Look at it,* he told himself, *red as blood.*

He walked away from the barn, walked until the shadows were tangled around his feet and it was hard to see the way. Wild horses couldn't have pulled him to the cabin. When it became so cold his body ached, he went back to the barn and burrowed into the hay and slept. When he awakened, it was dawn and some cattle were bawling outside. He got up, brushed stalks off his clothing and out of his hair, went out and fed, saw that the same steely sunlight was spreading, saddled up finally, and rode southerly. Bypassing the Muller place wasn't difficult. He leaned forward and let the horse run. He covered the distance to Tico in record time and left the trembling beast for the liveryman to cool out and care for.

There wasn't a soul in the saloon. The barman was cleaning shelves along the backbar. He gave Shan a drink and a long look, then went back to what he had been doing.

"Where is everybody?"

"Not many folks drink before breakfast," the barman replied.

"Give me another one."

He had four stiff drinks and went back outside. Across the way three men were holding up a wagon while the blacksmith wrestled a rear wheel close enough to hoist onto the spindle. Shan crossed the road and laughed aloud. The reddest-faced man looked up at him.

"What's so funny?" he demanded, looking mean.

"Three of you holding up a wagon," Shan replied, the liquor hot and pleasant in him. "Here, let me try it." He grasped the wagon under the tailgate and straightened his legs. The wagon went up several inches higher and a big vein in the side of Shan's head swelled, turned purple under the stress.

The blacksmith got the wheel on after three tries, and nodded. Shan let the wagon down and blinked away bursting lights that danced in front of his eyes.

No one said anything. The men moved off, and the smith was busy at the hub. Shan waited a moment, then went back across to the saloon. When he entered, the bartender and a thin man in a black frock coat were talking together. They both looked at him and fell silent. He ordered another shot and downed it. The man in the frock coat went out, and because it was so silent in the saloon, Shan said: "Who was that feller?"

"He's the sawbones hereabouts. His name's Jim Heath."

Doctor, a doctor. Shan put the cup down hard. *The* doctor. He went to the door and looked out. Dr. Heath was small in the distance, riding northwest. He was too far off. Shan went back and had another drink. "I wish I'd known that," he said. "I'd have stomped the whey out of him." The bartender looked at him but said nothing.

"He got an office in town?"

"Yes, south of here about a square, but he's hardly ever there. He goes out on calls at daybreak and don't get back sometimes until midnight."

"You're a friend of his, aren't you?"

"Doc's a fine fellow," the bartender said.

"And you're a damned liar, aren't you?"

The barman's mouth flattened a little but he said nothing.

"Telling me he won't be back. You know

damned well he'll be back and you're afraid I might be waiting for him, aren't you?"

"Listen, Shanley, Doc Heath makes a pretty big circuit. He usually stays overnight at the last place he makes a call. Tonight he won't be back at all. That's what he told me when he was in here, and that's what I been trying to tell you."

"How come you know my name?" Shan asked.

"That's not so hard. Tico's pretty small. There aren't a lot of folks in this country. Anyway, you're the fellow who whipped Tim O'Brien."

"Am I? Give me another shot then." He drank it and heard a roaring in his ears. "That's who I am, isn't it? The feller who knocked some sawdust out of Tim O'Brien." Shan leaned over the bar and lowered his voice. "That's not what you're thinking at all. You think I don't know? You're thinking I'm a squawman, that's what you're thinking, isn't it?"

"I don't know what you're talking about. Excuse me, I got to bring in some more bottles." The bartender moved swiftly around the end of the bar and disappeared through a door beyond. Shan was left alone. He looked at himself in the backbar mirror. His big black hat was dust- and sweat-streaked, its brim curled a little at the outer edges, a real up-and-at-'em Wyoming cowman in that mirror, shaggy head and all. He turned away. Sarahlee would cut his hair. No, not any more. No more haircuts. No more nothing, just squaws.

From now on just copper bottoms. Big ones, little ones, fat ones. When someone shook his arm, spoke to him, he didn't recognize the face or understand the words. He pulled away. "Who do you think you're pushing around, mister?"

"Shanley, you're drunk. It's kind of early in the day for serious drinking, isn't it?"

"Sure is. By golly, I know you now. The law-man. How are you anyway?"

"Well, I'm soberer than you are. Why don't you come down to my place and sleep it off?"

"I'm not sleepy."

"Come on. We'll get something to eat then. I'm sort of hungry myself."

He let the deputy marshal steer him to the dingy café where they sat and ate, drank coffee, talked, and drank more coffee. Shan was nearly sober when the lawman put a hand on his shoulder and got up.

"Take it easy, Shanley," he said quietly. "I don't know what's bothering you, but take it easy, pardner."

"Wait a minute," Shan said, getting up quickly. "Listen, I need some help."

The lawman walked toward the door with Shan trailing him. When they were outside, the deputy stopped. "Shanley," he said, "I've handled my share of drunks and I can read them like a book. The kind of help you need I can't give." He walked away.

CHAPTER NINETEEN

Shan got his horse from the livery barn and rode out of town northward. The ground was iron-hard underfoot, the sun kind of milky-looking. He went past the Muller place without looking in. He rode straight up the road to his own ranch like he had a hundred times, but he no longer felt like a king crossing his private empire. When he crossed the yard, he heard the cabin door open, but didn't look back. By the time he hung the saddle up his heart was beating almost normally. He peeked past the door, but she wasn't there, so he got the pitchfork and began feeding again, although it was scarcely noon. When he was finished with everything he could think to do, he went to the doorway and stood in it.

"Shan?"

He was startled because the voice hadn't come from the cabin area at all. She was standing over by the spring house.

"Hello, Sarahlee."

"Come over here."

The grayness of the wintry day didn't conceal any of her. All her bigness and her beauty were there for him to stare at. *You wait,* he told himself harshly, *you wait all your life for something like that, then you destroy it all in one blurry summer*. He crossed to her.

"Sit down here, Shan."

He sat on the edge of the spring box and said to himself: *Now she says I'm going home, Shan. You can have the ranch and the cattle and the horses and the little squaw. . . .*

"I talked to Mary, Shan."

Sure you did, Sarahlee. Please pull the damned trigger and get it over with because I'm bleeding inside. . . .

"We're going to keep her baby, Shan. We'll raise her child and mine both. I don't know of any other way."

"You hate me," he said. "I don't care about the kids. I really don't. I might, if things were different. Right now I don't. All I know is that you hate me."

She reached out and ran her hand up his shoulder to his cheek, smoothed the hair that hung down. "No, I don't Shan. I don't hate you. I don't know exactly what I feel for you but it isn't hate."

He turned toward her. "I don't give a damn *what* happens. I love you. I'll always love you."

She drew her hand back. "We aren't thinking about ourselves now, Shan, we're thinking about the children."

"Sure," he said, getting off the spring box.

"Mary and I had a long talk. We'll teach our children together. Teach them all the things mothers know and you'll teach them what fathers should teach them."

"Sure."

"Come on, Shan, supper's about ready." She led him by the arm, and just before they got to the cabin she said: "Act natural with Mary. She's frightened, Shan. Be pleasant with her."

He was. He was pleasant and polite and avoided her every chance he got, did not look into her face if he did not absolutely have to, and the next day he went silently to work on the porch, stayed with it until it was completed, then he began to make a long tier of firewood along the cabin wall under the porch's roof. He worked hard for days on end until he had all the wood they could possibly use for the entire winter, then out of sheer desperation and loneliness he rode down to the Muller place.

Otto was the same toward him as always. Mrs. Muller, who he didn't want to face but did, seemed only slightly less talkative than before but in all other ways the same. She had never been a loquacious person anyway. He rode down to see them often, and on one of those trips he met Tim O'Brien who was slogging up the road with some mail he'd picked up in Tico for the Mullers.

Shan didn't want to ride with him but he had no choice. Tim was polite. At the house Otto came out to greet them and his breath was like steam when he spoke. Tim didn't say ten words. When he left, he smiled down at Otto and Mrs. Muller and gave Shan a little nod.

After he was a dark speck on the road, Shan

said: "What's eating him now? I ate crow, didn't I?"

Mrs. Muller made a clucking sound. "Come on in by the stove, Shan, I've got some hot beef broth."

But he turned to Otto with a scowl and Otto nodded at his wife who closed the door softly and disappeared. Otto said: "There's a lot of talk going around, Shan."

"Don't these people have anything to do but mind other folks' business?"

"It isn't just Mary, Shan."

"What else?"

"The Blessing cattle, for one thing. Mary for another. A lot of the cowmen out here live alone, Shan."

"What of it?"

"Well, here you come along, a newcomer, and you got not one woman but two. It makes them hot under the collar thinking of you up there all winter with two women, boy."

Shan rammed fisted hands into the pockets of his big sheepskin coat. "Otto," he said quickly, "do you know what it's like up there with two women? They look at me like I'm a butcher's steer and at one another like they wished the damned floor'd open up and swallow somebody. They're so polite it makes me want to yell at them. You know who the luckiest person up there is . . . that buck Indian buried in the yard. He

246

doesn't hear or see a damned thing. Sometimes, when I'm in the cabin, I feel like the top of my head's going to explode. Otto, I've got to do something about this."

But he never did. He never had to because when the first big blizzard came Mary had a miscarriage. Shan was frightened sick while Sarahlee worked behind the curtain to save the girl. Then, when his terror dissolved, he noticed something. The tension was gone. The air inside the cabin was clean and pure again like it had been long before. For three days while Mary lay motionlessly in their bed, he and Sarahlee were close again. She even smiled at him as though she knew a solution to all their troubles had come, and she even cradled his head against her shoulder in Mary's pallet when they retired at night.

But that was a phase and Shan didn't know it. Sarahlee didn't, either. On the fifth night, Mary's condition reached a peak. Her dark eyes shone, hot and dry, and her lips were shriveled and cracked. Then the mirage collapsed, dissolved.

It was late the fifth night. They were in bed but not asleep. Shan heard her very plainly and it made his flesh crawl. The words were very distinct. Sarahlee, beside him in the narrow bed, stiffened. Mary was re-living her moments with Shan aloud. She was repeating the things they had said. It was terrible, lying there hearing it all so vividly.

Finally Sarahlee got up and said: "She's delirious."

Shan didn't move. He watched Sarahlee go to the water bucket, then back beyond the curtain, carrying a basin of water.

The words kept rising and falling until Sarahlee broke the fever with cold water. For a while there was utter silence, then Mary began speaking again, mumbling, but this time in her native tongue and Shan wanted to yell at her: *Why didn't you use that a half hour ago, damn you!*

Sarahlee laid down beside Mary on the bed behind the curtain. Shan heard the bed groan under the added weight. He closed his eyes and tried to sleep, but it was useless, so he crooked his arms under his head and stared at the ceiling, heard the coyotes, caught the rise of a little wind that whimpered along the pole rafters, rustled over the roof, and fled southward. Sarahlee did not return to his side that night.

At 5:00 the next morning, when it was bitter cold in the cabin and as dark as pitch, Sarahlee spoke to him. She hadn't been asleep, either. Each word was as clear as struck glass. The longest night in their lives had come to an end.

"Shan. Mary is dead."

He laid there with an echo that didn't exist repeating itself in his mind.

Then Sarahlee spoke again: "Go outside, Shan."

He got up, pulled his clothes on, and went out into the freezing darkness. He saw the clear, merciless stare of a million stars and began walking across the yard to the barn. He forked feed to the animals, that looked at him, round-eyed and blank. Forked more feed to them than they'd need all day long. It was movement. It was action. A solitary bead of sweat ran down his nose and hung there until he shook his head.

Then he got the pick, the crowbar, and a shovel, and went over where the unknown buck Indian's grave was and began to tear at the frozen ground. The pick made a high sound when he drove it into the earth, high and flat. He worried up chunks of earth and sweat burst out all over him. He got past the frost at six inches. After that it was easier and he kept right on digging. When it got light in the sky, there was a sickly pale iridescence to the world. Snow weather.

The grave grew steadily deeper. Finally he pulled himself out of it and stood there with his teeth chattering and sweating at the same time. The world was absolutely without sound. He went to the cabin and pushed the door inward. The first thing he noticed was that the blanket that had always formed the partition around the bed was gone. Sarahlee was sitting by the stove in a chair. She was fully clothed. Mary lay on the bed. Her hair had been brushed until it shone glossy black and she was wearing the beaded buckskin dress. The curtain was wrapped around her, all but the face and shoulders.

From over by the stove Sarahlee said: "So you could see her face. Did you make the grave?"

"Yes."

"Carry her out."

He gathered Mary into his arms and didn't look at her face. At the door he hesitated.

"I'm going to stay in here," Sarahlee said. "I'll pray."

He buried Mary. It took a long time, more sweat, but he didn't notice this time. The clouds scudded, low and heavy, overhead. When he was finished, he put the tools away, and lingered in the barn for a little while, walking around, looking at the animals, listening to them eating. He stopped in front of the yellow-wheeled buggy for a moment, then he went across the yard to the cabin, stooped to pick up an armload of wood and take it in with him, dumping it into the woodbox by the stove. He used the lifter to open the firebox, saw that the embers were glowing low, and put in more wood. After he'd closed the firebox door, he looked at Sarahlee. She hadn't moved. He crossed to the table and dropped down there. Her chestnut hair lay softly wavy down the back of her head, past her shoulders.

"Shan, *that*'s between us. I guess I knew it always would be. I guess I just wouldn't face it because I loved you. It's there between me and my love for you . . . I told myself you couldn't help yourself, that you were so big and strong . . . that you had to have release. That might have stood up for me over the years, Shan, I don't know. But it was wrong, of course, and we both knew that. Maybe she did, too. I thought it might come out all right, though. Not now. Not with her death between us. We couldn't do it now, Shan, no matter what we told ourselves."

Sarahlee got up. Until then he hadn't noticed that she had their Bible in her hands. She put it back on the shelf by the bed, then she went to the stove with her back to him.

"Go hitch up the buggy, Shan."

He went without a question, harnessed the mare, backed her between the shafts, buckled her in, and stood beside the buggy in the wintry yard while inside him something crumbled away. When he heard the cabin door open and close, he looked up. Sarahlee had her heavy hat and coat on. Her hands were buried in mittens. She passed in front of him, climbed up to the seat, and took the lines.

"Where will you go?" he said.

She didn't answer the question. "You can get the buggy in Tico. I'll leave it at the livery barn." She said other things he hardly heard. It was like they were being shouted to him from an impossible distance; things like having her child born in a hospital among people she knew, that her child would have things, find opportunities. Finally he broke into the flow of words, tried to move and stand so that she would have to look at him.

"I want our baby to have everything, Sarahlee. I'll send you all the money I can as soon as I sell some cattle."

"No, the greatest favor you can do this child is never come into its life. If you do, it will have to know about you someday. That would be the worst thing a child could know."

"I'm its father, Sarahlee."

"It has no father," she said, lifting the lines. "Its father is dead. He was a soldier and he is dead." She flipped the lines and the mare began to crunch over the frozen earth.

He stood in the yard until she was lost to sight, then he went inside without looking at the tamped clods, the raw upturned earth, poured a cup of whiskey, and drank it. The cabin shrieked with silence, with emptiness, with pain, and finally with death. Life in Wyoming had blinked out that quickly.

About the Author

Lauran Paine who, under his own name and various pseudonyms has written over a thousand books, was born in Duluth, Minnesota. His family moved to California when he was at a young age and his apprenticeship as a Western writer came about through the years he spent in the livestock trade, rodeos, and even motion pictures where he served as an extra because of his expert horsemanship in several films starring movie cowboy Johnny Mack Brown. In the late 1930s, Paine trapped wild horses in northern Arizona and even, for a time, worked as a professional farrier. Paine came to know the Old West through the eyes of many who had been born in the previous century, and he learned that Western life had been very different from the way it was portrayed on the screen. "I knew men who had killed other men," he later recalled. "But they were the exceptions. Prior to and during the Depression, people were just too busy eking out an existence to indulge in Saturday-night brawls." He served in the U.S. Navy in the Second World War and began writing for Western pulp magazines following his discharge. It is interesting to note that all of his earliest novels (written under his own name and the pseudonym

Mark Carrel) were published in the British market and he soon had as strong a following in that country as in the United States. Paine's Western fiction is characterized by strong plots, authenticity, an apparently effortless ability to construct situation and character, and a preference for building his stories upon a solid foundation of historical fact. *Adobe Empire* (1956), one of his best novels, is a fictionalized account of the last twenty years in the life of trader William Bent and, in an off-trail way, has a melancholy, bittersweet texture that is not easily forgotten. In later novels like *The White Bird* (1997) and *Cache Cañon* (1998), he showed that the special magic and power of his stories and characters had only matured along with his basic themes of changing times, changing attitudes, learning from experience, respecting Nature, and the yearning for a simpler, more moderate way of life.

Center Point Large Print
600 Brooks Road / PO Box 1
Thorndike, ME 04986-0001 USA

(207) 568-3717

**US & Canada:
1 800 929-9108**
www.centerpointlargeprint.com